Acclaim for the authors of

in Paris

BARBARA BRETTON

"One of today's best women's fiction authors."
—*The Romance Reader*

"A master storyteller..."
—*Booklist*

MARIE FERRARELLA

"*Finding Home* is wonderful, filled with humor
and heart. The picture of a husband who
means well but hasn't a clue is dead-on."
—*Romantic Times BOOKreviews*

"This book will keep the reader firmly engaged
until the final page."
—*Romantic Times BOOKreviews* on
Sundays Are for Murder

CINDI MYERS

Myers's ability to portray true-to-life sympathetic characters
ill resonate most with readers of this captivating romance."
—*Publishers Weekly* on *Learning Curves*

"Delightful and delicious...
Cindi Myers always satisfies!"
—*USA TODAY* bestselling author Julie Ortolon

ABOUT THE AUTHORS

BARBARA BRETTON

Barbara Bretton wanted to be a writer from the moment she was old enough to hold a pencil. What could be better than spending all day with your imaginary friends and getting paid for it? She sold her first book (longer ago than she cares to admit) to Harlequin American Romance and was delighted when *Love Changes* went on to be a launch title. Even though she has written and published over forty novels since then, she remains deeply grateful (and a bit surprised) to find herself living her childhood dream.

MARIE FERRARELLA

Born in West Germany, educated in New York City and now happily thriving in California, Marie Ferrarella, *USA TODAY* bestselling author of 191 books and counting, began pounding out stories on an old manual Remington typewriter her mother bought her from a pawn shop when she was ten years old. She cannot remember a time when she didn't want to write. One of her greatest joys in life is entertaining people and making them laugh. This RITA® Award-winning mother of two and wife of one hopes to be buried with her computer. Her last words will probably be "Wait, wait, I still have one more story left to write."

CINDI MYERS

Cindi Myers had a French pen pal in high school and spent a wonderful sixteen days with the family the summer after her graduation. Unfortunately, all she saw of Paris was the airport. She hopes to return to the City of Light one day. In the meantime, she indulges herself with French pastry, chocolate and wine and romantic daydreams like the ones that inspired this story.

Barbara Bretton

Marie Ferrarella

Cindi Myers

A Wedding in Paris

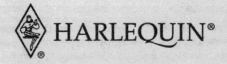

HARLEQUIN®

TORONTO • NEW YORK • LONDON
AMSTERDAM • PARIS • SYDNEY • HAMBURG
STOCKHOLM • ATHENS • TOKYO • MILAN • MADRID
PRAGUE • WARSAW • BUDAPEST • AUCKLAND

ISBN-13: 978-0-373-83712-0
ISBN-10:   0-373-83712-7

A WEDDING IN PARIS

Copyright © 2007 by Harlequin Books S. A.

The publisher acknowledges the copyright holders of the individual works as follows:

WE'LL ALWAYS HAVE PARIS
Copyright © 2007 by Barbara Bretton

SOMETHING BORROWED, SOMETHING BLUE
Copyright © 2007 by Marie Rydzynski-Ferrarella

PICTURE PERFECT
Copyright © 2007 by Cynthia Myers

This edition published by arrangement with Harlequin Books S.A.

® and TM are trademarks of the publisher. Trademarks indicated with ® are registered in the United States Patent and Trademark Office, the Canadian Trade Marks Office and in other countries.

www.eHarlequin.com

Printed in U.S.A.

CONTENTS

WE'LL ALWAYS HAVE PARIS

Barbara Bretton

To Tina and Marsha with thanks

PROLOGUE

The Engagement Party
Long Island—winter

LAUGHTER SPILLED out of the big yellow house at the end of Meadow Run Road. Curls of smoke rose from the chimney and spun upward toward the moon, which hung full and glowing in the ink-black sky. The promise of more snow was in the air, but that hadn't kept anyone away. Cars filled the driveway, part of the front lawn, the street.

"Shh!" she whispered as they slipped deeper into the shadowy backyard where their girls had played as children. "They'll hear us."

He pulled her close and she melted into his embrace. "I don't plan on doing a lot of talking, do you?"

She shivered and this time it wasn't from the winter chill that blanketed the northeast. "No talking," she agreed. Even though not talking was what had gotten them into trouble.

But who needed words when the moon was full

and the champagne tasted like starlight? There was nothing like your daughter's engagement party to remind you that once upon a time you had believed in happy endings, too. Romance was everywhere. The house was filled with music and laughter. The people they loved most in the world were gathered together to celebrate the wonders of love. You couldn't help believing in forever on a night like this.

He smelled the way she remembered, of spice and heat and mountain lakes. He had laughed the first time she told him that. *You're a Long Island girl,* he had reminded her. *What do you know from mountain lakes?* But she knew wonderful when she saw it and for a long, long time what they had together was very wonderful.

He took her hand and they darted around the weather-beaten shed where the girls had stowed their bicycles another lifetime ago. Hard snow crackled like glass beneath their feet. She slipped on a patch of ice, but his strong arms caught her before she hit the ground. He had never let her fall, not once.

Not even now, at the end.

He didn't ask why she had stopped having the driveway salted.

She didn't remind him that they didn't live there anymore; their youngest daughter and her roommates did.

This was a moment out of time. Nothing before this moment existed. Nothing after it would matter.

There was only the two of them.

He opened the passenger door of his rental car and they scrambled inside.

"A Toyota?" she asked, brow raised.

"They were fresh out of '74 Cutlasses."

Her sigh filled the tiny space. "I haven't thought about your dad's Cutlass in years."

"I have." He unzipped his jacket and drew her inside its warmth. "We should have had it declared a national monument."

How many hours had they spent in the back seat of that big blue car, young and wildly in love, burning with the kind of fever only the other's touch could ease.

"They're so young," she whispered against his neck. "I hope they know what they're doing."

"We had three children when we were their age," he reminded her.

"It's a different world today. We were—" She shrugged inside his embrace. How did you describe a sense of inevitability that shook you right through to your marrow?

"Crazy," he whispered against her hair.

"Fearless," she whispered against his neck.

"They're in love," he said as he did magical things to the length of her spine. "Alexis is following her heart."

"Like we did," she said.

"Like we did," he agreed.

Except for the fact that they were on the fast track to divorce, it would have been a great story to tell their future grandchildren.

Less than a week ago Alexis had shown up with a handsome man by her side and a big announcement to make. She and Gabe Fellini planned to be married in early spring in Paris.

Just wait until you see Paris, Alexis had raved as she shared her news. *I don't know why you and Daddy never traveled anywhere.*

Her darling daughter hadn't a clue what she was asking of them.

Paris was their city, their secret dream for as long as Kate could remember. High-school sweethearts, they were going to run away together to the City of Light as soon as they graduated. They would put college on hold, grab backpacks and whatever savings they could scrape up, and set out to conquer the world. Ryan would write the Great American Novel while she followed in the footsteps of Monet and Renoir and Sargent.

One day in the far-distant future they would settle down and raise a family, but not until they had had their fill of Paris.

But there was one slight flaw in their plan: a baby daughter named Shannon who arrived eight months after graduation.

And even though they were painfully careful,

another baby daughter named Alexis had shown up less than two years later.

And seven years into their marriage, just when they thought they could put the diapers and burping blankets and binkies away for good, Taylor joined them.

In the blink of an eye they had gone from love-struck teenagers to loving parents without a chance to slow down and catch their breath. Life didn't work that way. Life didn't slow down and make allowances for youthful enthusiasm, for sweet mistakes, for the daily struggles every couple faced. The only thing you could do was run as fast as you could and hope you'd catch up with each other somewhere down the line.

Through it all, there was always Paris. *One day,* they promised each other when times were tough and life seemed to be plotting against them. One day when the kids were grown they would make that dream come true.

Who could have guessed their middle child would be the one to make it happen?

Who would have guessed it would be too late?

"Paris," Kate murmured against his mouth.

"Paris," he said and then, for a long time, they didn't say anything at all.

CHAPTER ONE

Paris—the following spring
Six days before the wedding

"MERCI." Kate Finney Donovan fumbled with the fistful of euros then finally handed them all to the impossibly good-looking bellman waiting expectantly by the door. *"Merci beaucoup."*

He bowed and said either, "May I be the father of your children?" or "Lady, you'd better take a crash course in the exchange rate," then closed the door behind him.

She laughed for the first time in eighteen hours of traffic jams, airport security checks, turbulence, and just plain mother-of-the-bride jitters.

Clearly it was a testament to the Parisians that she had made it from the airport to the hotel without incident and with most of her money still in her wallet. She had relied on the kindness of English-speaking cab drivers and her memory of high-school French to keep her from going too far astray and neither had let her down. Although, judging by the bellman's reaction to the tip she had given him, maybe she had better reread the section on currency in *Paris for Tourists* before bed.

She was staying in the apartment her great-aunt Celeste Beaulieu kept at the Hotel St. Michel on the Left Bank. Celeste was already at the inn named Milles Fleurs, which was located on the outskirts of the city, for the wedding festivities, and she had suggested Kate might want to spend a few days in pampered luxury before the wedding craziness got into full swing.

Celeste knew all about her lapse of sanity the night of the engagement party. She had listened as Kate poured out her heart a few days later, held Kate's hand across the transatlantic wires as she alternately blamed herself then Ryan for thinking with their hormones and not their heads. Only Celeste knew what Paris had meant to them and how hard it would be to see the city for the first time as one-half of an about-to-be-divorced couple.

"You will do as I say, *chérie,*" Celeste had commanded, as only a Frenchwoman from Brooklyn could. "Send on your bags to Milles Fleurs and tell Alexis that you have business to attend elsewhere before you can join them."

"You want me to lie to her?" Kate had asked, warming to the idea despite herself.

"The business is your heart." What Celeste apparently wanted was for Kate to discover Paris in her own way, on her own time, so that she would have some control of her emotions when she finally saw Ryan again. Perhaps if she got all of those Paris "firsts" out of the way she would stand a fighting chance.

Considering the fact that she'd burst into tears at her first glimpse of the Eiffel Tower, her aunt might have a point. Even through the thick fog of jet lag, the City of Light's staggering beauty had overwhelmed her as she rode in from the airport. It was every bit as dazzling as she had imagined it as a giddy teenager in love with love and dying for romance. Wide boulevards. Narrow cobblestone streets. Graceful trees dressed in the lacy greens of spring. The Eiffel Tower rising up into the late-morning sky like a dream.

She could almost see the ghosts of Renoir and Monet, Hemingway and Fitzgerald watching over the young artists and writers who sat hunched over sketch pads and laptops and steaming bowls of onion soup, feasting on every wonderful thing the city had to offer.

Why didn't we do this years ago, Ryan? Before it was too late for us....

She already knew the answer. Children happened. Careers happened. Life happened. And somewhere along the way dreams faded.

Thank God, she had listened to Celeste and claimed this time for herself. Her bags were safely en route to Milles Fleurs. Her daughters thought she was meeting with a gallery owner who was staying in a farmhouse in the Loire Valley.

All she had with her was an overnight bag, some toiletries, and the family portrait she had painted at her daughter's request. Somehow her daughter's request had validated her growing success as a portrait artist in a way her many commissions never had. Had Celeste known that traveling light would make her feel glamorous and sophisticated, like one of those world travelers who could put everything they needed in a duffel bag and have room to spare for tchotchkes? More than likely. When it came to life, eighty-something Celeste Beaulieu pretty much had it all figured out.

Celeste was Kate's grandmother's older sister who had moved to France in the 1950s, married a handsome Frenchman, and never looked back. She was one of those women who seemed born with an understanding of the inner workings of romance, a throwback to the days of salons and gentlemen callers. Celeste understood without being told that the combination of Parisian charm and Alexis's wedding might be more than a woman on the verge of divorce could handle.

The sitting room was elegant and quintessentially French. An antique armoire that would have been at home in the Louvre bumped shoulders with an angularly modern chair reminiscent of

Vladimir Kagan. The sitting room opened into a library, which led to the bedroom in the rear of the apartment. The bed was short but invitingly wide, a frothy confection of heavenly pillows and down-filled duvets of dove-gray silk shot through with mauve as seductive as a secret lover.

Long casement windows overlooked the wide street below and, just beyond, the legendary Seine made its way to the sea. Once upon a time the hotel had been a haven for young artists and Kate's sharp eye caught faint smears of phthalo-green and alizarin-crimson on the sill.

"I'm in Paris," she said out loud to the empty room and waited for the rush of excitement she'd been expecting since her plane landed.

To her dismay, despite the beauty all around her, she might as well have been in Philadelphia.

It was the timing.

Who would have thought the Fates would conspire to grant her fondest wish two weeks before she and Ryan signed the papers that would officially mark the end of thirty years of marriage? Apparently fate had a twisted sense of humor, but for once Kate wasn't laughing. Paris was everything it was supposed to be and more, but Ryan wasn't there to share it with Kate and that made all the difference.

It took her a moment to realize the telephone on the escritoire was ringing.

"Bienvenu, chérie!" Celeste said when Kate answered. Celeste was truly ageless. She still retained the enthusiasm of a twenty-year-old-girl. "I have been phoning for two hours now. You had a safe trip?"

Kate rapped her knuckles against the mahogany table. "Knock wood. Slow but safe."

"And you are settled into the apartment?"

"It's beautiful," Kate enthused. "I can't thank you enough."

Celeste made one of those Gallic sounds that could mean just about anything. "And what are your plans for the day?"

Good question. Everyone said traveling west to east was easy, but she felt as if she had spent the flight strapped to the wheel well. "I guess I'll order up some room service and take a nap. Try to get myself adjusted to the time change."

"Mais non!"

"Mais oui," she countered, laughing. "I'm not as young as you, Aunt Celeste. I need a nap before I go sightseeing."

"A nap!" Celeste's outrage was formidable. "I forbid you to nap. You're in Paris, *chérie.* You can nap in New York. Comb your hair. Put on fresh lipstick. That's all you need."

Maybe that was all Celeste needed, but Kate's list was growing longer by the second with caffeine in the top position.

They chatted a few minutes about the wedding. Neither one mentioned Ryan, which was fine with Kate although he was clearly the blue suede elephant in the room. Alexis and Gabe had talked to Celeste last winter and the family matriarch had bestowed her seal of approval on the match.

That didn't surprise Kate at all. Gabe Fellini was everything Kate could have asked for in a son-in-law. With Aunt Celeste's help, he and Alexis had arranged the entire wedding festivities with flawless precision and so far there hadn't been a ripple of discontent from anyone involved.

The extended Fellini and Donovan families were crazy about one another. Alexis's sisters Shannon and Taylor had happily granted the middle child her day in the sun. And the only thing required of the mother of the bride was that she show up a few days before the Big Day with her dress and the family portrait she had promised them on the night of their engagement party.

Which was otherwise known as the night she lost her mind.

There was no other way to explain what had happened. Not even to herself. It was as if her body had been taken over by an alien being whose sole purpose was to leap into that Toyota and have her way with Ryan.

When the girls told her, so very gently, that their father had said he was bringing someone with him to the party, Kate had steeled herself for the sight of another woman at her husband's side. He was a gorgeous man. Sooner or later he was going to realize there was a world of women out there and he could have his pick.

She was braced for a twenty-year-old bimbo with fake breasts, porcelain veneers, and thighs the likes of which Kate could only dream about.

But it didn't happen that way. Long Island's snowstorm had moved north and flights between Boston, where Ryan hosted a successful sports radio show, and New York had been cancelled.

Kate was ashamed of the quick surge of relief she experienced when she realized she would be spared the sight of him with another woman.

"We can't have this party without Daddy here," Alexis had said, but Kate had been firm in her resolve.

"He told you to go ahead without him and he meant it, honey. Your father wouldn't want you to cancel your engagement party because he couldn't get a flight down."

In a world of change, the one constant was Ryan's love for his daughters. He wanted the best for them and would do anything to make sure they got it.

About an hour into the party, Kate was carrying a tray of shrimp appetizers into the living room when she heard familiar laughter ringing out in the front hallway.

Ryan had rented a car at Logan Airport and driven down to Long Island through the storm to be there to celebrate his daughter's engagement. Kate thought her heart would burst through her chest from longing when she first caught sight of him in the foyer. Snowflakes glittered in his hair beneath the overhead light. He laughed as he brushed them off and handed his scarf and jacket to a beaming bride-to-be.

"Mom, look!" Alexis said as Kate stepped into the room. "Daddy drove all the way down through the blizzard to be here with us."

"I thought you were bringing someone," Kate said.

Ryan frowned. "Where'd you get that idea?"

They both turned to look at their middle child, who looked back with an innocent smile on her face. She wasn't fooling anyone.

"I hope you rented a four-wheel drive," Kate said to Ryan. *What had happened to Hello or It's good to see you? Why did she have to go straight to the negative.*

"I'm crazy, but I don't have a death wish," he shot back. "I rented an all-wheel drive at the airport."

"There's a blizzard out there," she pointed out.

"That's not a blizzard," he said. "You need higher winds to qualify as a blizzard."

"That's still an awful lot of snow." *Shut up, Kate. Where is this going? What's the point?*

"It was clear sailing from Hartford on. The worst is on its way to Maine."

Kate opened her mouth to pursue this meteorological debate, but the look on their daughter's face stopped her.

Alexis was looking from Kate to Ryan, her blue eyes wide with puzzlement. This was her day. Kate and Ryan could save their bickering for some other time.

That look of puzzlement quickly turned into something very different when Gabe Fellini walked into the room.

There was something both sad and beautiful about new love. Alexis and Gabe were so innocent, so trusting in their love for each other. They hadn't a clue about the curveballs life would throw their way. Right now they believed that they were special, that the gods had decided to rain down all the blessings of the universe on their heads and protect them always from harm.

She and Ryan had been that way, too, and for a second Kate thought she was looking at their younger selves.

And Ryan saw it, too. Their gazes locked above their daughter's head and everything else fell away. The years. The problems. The fact that they were a half step away from finalizing their divorce.

They exchanged a smile in the foyer. They squeezed past each other in the back hallway. She smiled when she caught him watching her as she popped more crab puffs into the oven. She blushed furiously when he caught her peeking at him through the back window when he stepped outside to bring in some more firewood.

By the time they found themselves alone on the back porch, the attraction between them was so powerful that they were in each other's arms in the space of a heartbeat.

He told her what he wanted to do to her.

She told him if he didn't do it in the next thirty seconds she would do it to him.

In a flash they were in the backseat of the Toyota with the windows fogging up all around them. Hot. Sweet. Intense.

Too intense. She was losing control and if she didn't get out of there right that second she would say something she would regret. Something like *I still love you* or *Maybe we should give it another try*, and she would have to endure the look of pity in his eyes.

Kate scrambled into her clothes as if the car were on fire and she had ten seconds to save her own life.

Which, come to think of it, may not have been that far from the truth.

She had made a big fat mistake. One of those mistakes that happened to other, dumber women who ended up crying their eyes out on some relationship expert's shoulder on national television.

She hadn't planned to sleep with her own

husband. It was winter, for crying out loud. She hadn't even shaved her legs.

For three weeks afterward she held her breath, praying to God and all the saints that their stupidity hadn't resulted in a middle-aged pregnancy. She had the feeling Ryan heard her sigh of relief all the way up there in Boston.

Not that they had had any direct communication since the engagement party. They had been hiding behind Alexis and their lawyers, passing messages back and forth like grade-school kids behind their teacher's back.

If their daughters ever got wind of what had happened, they would immediately jump to the wrong conclusion. Her children were adults, but they clung to the childish hope that their parents would somehow get back together.

She had bumped into Alexis as she ran upstairs after the incident in the Toyota. Kate had been wild with emotion, almost crazy. She had yanked her wedding ring off her finger and flung it into the deepest recesses of the top drawer of her old dresser. It wasn't until she turned around and saw her middle child standing in the doorway looking both puzzled and horrified that she managed to pull in the reins on her romantic craziness and settle back down into being the mother of the bride.

She thought about the ring sometimes, but she had yet to drive back out to the house and retrieve it. There was always something else to do, somewhere else she needed to be. She knew she could ask Taylor to FedEx it to her but she hadn't done that yet either.

Maybe there was something symbolic about tossing the ring into the darkness of a forgotten drawer. At first she had felt naked without her ring, but after a while she grew used to the feeling. Maybe she should gather up all of those old, troublesome memories and throw them into the darkness with the ring and be done with all of it.

The truth was that fiery interlude in the rental car hadn't changed a thing between them. The wheels of divorce kept on rolling as the weeks slipped away. In fact, they could have signed the final papers yesterday before she flew out of New York but somehow it didn't seem right for parents to end their marriage one week before their daughter's wedding.

Weddings were about living happily ever after. Nobody wanted a reminder that sometimes not even love was enough to keep two people together.

She wouldn't be able to avoid him once Wedding Week began. That much was certain. They would walk their daughter down the aisle together. They would pose for pictures together. They would step out onto the dance floor together as the parents of the bride.

Temptation would be everywhere, but this time she would be prepared.

She would stay away from champagne, hide indoors when the moon was high and bright in the sky, and she would definitely stay away from rented Toyotas and the men who drove them.

But it had been so wonderful to see him again at the party...to share a secret smile as they toasted their daughter's happiness...to melt into his arms as she had in the beginning when it was all new and wonderful and Paris still beckoned them like a glittering golden dream....

Laughter drifted up from the bistro on the corner and carried with it the intoxicating scents of old dark Gauloises, buttery onions and wine so deep and red it stained your lips when you drank it. If she closed her eyes and blocked out the traffic and the laughter, she could almost hear the wistful notes of *La Vie en Rose.*

She brought herself up short. These trips down memory lane were getting her nowhere but depressed.

She was in Paris, the most beautiful city in the world, and she wasn't going to waste time mooning over the past. Who needed romance when she could window-shop Chanel?

But first things first. If she was going to enjoy every minute, she needed a long shower, a huge pot of strong black coffee and an obscene amount of freshly baked goodies.

The women she had noticed on the way into the

city from the airport had all been slim and amazingly stylish. She could only hope it had something to do with pastries.

CHAPTER TWO

AS IT TURNED OUT, the number-one footballer in England wasn't big on interviews and Ryan was finished in less time than it took to eat a Big Mac with fries. The superstar's answers were, in random order, *yes, no, I dunno* and a firm *maybe*. Good thing the guy had been given a hard head and a great right foot, because clearly conversation wasn't his strong suit. But the most important words, "I'm retiring at the end of the season" had come through loud and clear.

Why Derek Brody chose to hand that exclusive to an American was Celeste Beaulieu's secret. How his aunt-in-law even knew Brody was a mystery for the ages, but when she phoned Ryan in Boston and asked if he wanted a sit-down interview with the elusive sports star he didn't have to think twice.

"You caught him on a good day," one of the photographers said as they left the hotel suite after the interview. "The bloke's not always that chatty."

Ryan was still laughing when he reached the other side of the Channel.

Originally he had figured to spend a day or two in London before he joined the rest of the family at Milles Fleurs for the start of Wedding Week.

"I might stick around town," he told Aunt Celeste over the phone yesterday. "Look up some old friends."

Celeste, however, was nobody's fool. She was the only person on the planet who understood what Paris meant to him and to Kate.

And why he was trying to stay away as long as he could.

"Hair of the dog, *mon cher.* Immerse yourself in my city now, before you see Kate again. London will always be there waiting for you. Now it is time for Paris."

What was it about the French anyway? Celeste was French by choice, not blood, but when it came to understanding love, she might as well have been born on the banks of the Seine. He hadn't told anyone about what had happened at the engagement party, but the old woman's romance radar had honed in on the change in the status quo with unerring precision.

"Never underestimate our Kate," she had counseled him. "Her truest feelings are the ones she shields from view."

Apparently she hadn't managed to shield some of those truest feelings from Alexis on that fateful night. He had received an impassioned e-mail from their daughter the next day, chronicling the sight of her mother flinging her wedding band into a dresser drawer in what used to be their bedroom.

Why does it have to be this way? Alexis had written in her e-mail. *You two were always so happy together. Why can't love last the way it's supposed to?*

Four months later he was still looking for the answer to that question.

So now there he was in the lobby of the Hotel St. Michel on the Left Bank, trying to explain to the concierge that they were welcome to take his bags up to Madame Beaulieu's suite but he wouldn't be going with them.

Back home his French didn't sound half-bad. He had no trouble ordering off the menu at any French restaurant between New York and Boston. Here in Paris he sounded like a not-too-bright four-year-old with a limited vocabulary.

"*Le bistro,*" he said, gesturing toward the corner restaurant he'd noticed when he got out of the cab. "*Déjeuner.*" He mimed repeatedly raising a spoon to his lips. "*Bon appétit!*"

He had to hand it to the concierge. The guy didn't crack a smile. He nodded and said, "Your bags will be in your suite when you return," in perfect English.

"Thanks," Ryan muttered, not even attempting a pathetic *merci.* He pocketed the room key and was out the door before anybody else tried to start a conversation with him.

Kate would have laughed until she cried. She would have teased him in that gentle way of hers, forcing him to see the humor in the situation. Even during the darkest times, she had known how to make him laugh.

God, how he missed her laughter.

So why haven't you called her, Donovan? It's been four months....

He wasn't going to finish that thought. He'd been trying—and failing—to forget what happened between them in his rented Toyota. It wasn't his finest hour, but he'd be damned if he knew exactly why. You would think a man his age would have learned something along the way, but that night he found out how little he knew about women.

About Kate.

They had been curled together in that ridiculous little backseat when she bolted. One second they were lying together, waiting for their heartbeats to slow down to something even close to normal, and the next she was scrambling into her clothes like a crazed contortionist. One of her practical jokes, he was sure of it, designed to defuse the emotions of the moment. He reached for her, expecting her to start laughing that beautiful laugh of hers, when she flung open the passenger door and leaped out. The last time he saw Kate, she was fleeing across the snowy driveway like an Olympic speed skater going for the gold.

A bucketful of ice water over his head couldn't have been more effective in bringing him back down to earth.

Which was where he had pretty much been ever since.

He almost called her a thousand times. He'd punch in the speed-dial number on his cell phone and the second it rang he'd hang up like a teenage boy with a crush on the head cheerleader. Young people make stupid, careless mistakes. You weren't supposed to make those same mistakes when you were well into your forties. Somewhere along the way you should have learned something about caution and responsibility.

But when it came to Kate, in many ways he was still the same kid who had fallen in love with her back in the sophomore year of high school. He was the jock who secretly wanted to write. She was the math whiz who longed to be an artist. They had nothing in common and yet they had everything. The fact that they found each other so early always seemed like a miracle to him, the best gift God could have sent his way.

But somewhere, somehow, they had managed to lose track of each other. A man and woman could live in the same house, eat at the same table, sleep in the same bed for years and never see it happening. One day you turn around and nothing looks familiar, not your place in the world, not even the woman you loved.

He nodded at the doorman as he stepped onto the sidewalk. Laughter rang out from the corner bistro. A street musician played something unrecognizable on an old violin while a pair of young lovers nuzzled nearby. The air was redolent of garlic and wine and cigarette smoke, of river water and old books.

It was everything he always imagined it would be, this dream city, and he didn't feel a damn thing beyond the need for a cup of coffee and something to eat.

The corner bistro didn't look bad even if they did seem to seat as many dogs as humans. A huge Newfoundland dozed near his master's feet at one of the sidewalk tables while a fluffy white poodle flaunted her superiority from a window seat inside. A chalkboard menu rested on an easel to the right of the front door. He stepped closer. *Boeuf.* Okay, that was a gimme. Maybe a steak? A burger? *Poulet* was chicken, but he couldn't tell what they were doing with the chicken. He was scanning for something familiar like French fries when the word *omelette* jumped out at him. He liked eggs. Like most men, he could eat breakfast any hour of the day. Besides, you couldn't screw up an egg.

He did a double take. Did that say *fish omelet?*

Nobody ate fish omelets. He knew that he'd probably screwed something in the translation, but he wasn't going to take a chance. They had Golden Arches in Paris, didn't they? Maybe he would take the easy way out for his first meal and sample the local cuisine later.

The Eiffel Tower seemed as good a direction as any and he was about to head out when he caught sight of a woman sitting at a small round table near the window. He couldn't see her face, but there was something about her that tugged at his heart. Kate's hair was crazy curly like that, too. It dipped across her cheek when she bent her head and caught the sunlight the same way.

Impossible. Kate wasn't due at Milles Fleurs for another two days. She was probably back home in New York raiding Barney's for the perfect mother-of-the-bride outfit.

"...*vers la droite!*" a voice behind him called out.

His mind went blank. Was *droite* left or right? He moved to the right just in time to keep from being knocked over by a young woman on bright red roller skates. An apple-cheeked baby smiled at him from a backpack as they sailed past.

By the time he turned back to the bistro window, the woman with the crazy headful of curls was gone.

C'est la vie, he thought, chalking it up to imagination and caffeine withdrawal. A mirage. It made sense that Kate would be uppermost in his mind.

She was the woman who had dreamed this dream with him for as long as he could remember.

The curly strawberry-blond hair. The way she ducked her head when she took a bite of food. The blue topaz pendant dangling from a slender chain around her neck.

He burst into the bistro like a madman. The hostess, a woman of great style and indeterminate age, stepped in front of him. Immovable object, meet the irresistible force.

She said something to him in French that he didn't understand.

He said something to her in French that neither one of them understood.

She glanced about and he had the distinct feeling she was about to call for security.

"La femme," he said, pointing toward the empty table next to the window. *"Cheveux rouges…"* He twirled his index finger in the air. What the hell was the French word for *curly? "Bouclés!"* You would think he had split the atom. *"La femme avec les cheveux rouges bouclés."*

Contact! The woman's face relaxed into a wide smile and she led him to the table where he'd seen the woman he now wasn't so sure was Kate after all. A half-eaten bowl of onion soup sat atop the scarred wooden tabletop. A wineglass with a smudge of peach lipstick along the rim. Kate didn't drink red wine. Or did she?

The hostess motioned for him to sit down. He hesitated. What the hell had he gotten himself into? A strange woman was going to walk back to the table and see some nutty American guy sitting there and probably call for a *gendarme.*

But the hostess was beaming a smile at him and people were looking, so he sat down on the bentwood chair and smiled his thanks when a busboy handed him a small, handwritten menu.

The thing to do was get up and leave before the woman came back to reclaim her seat. There was an exit near the bathroom. All he had to do was stand up, head for the bathroom, then detour out the door before he was arrested for stalking.

He pushed back his chair and stood up. Nobody noticed. He casually walked in the direction of the bathroom. Nobody paid any attention. He was less than six feet from the exit when the bathroom door swung open and he found himself face-to-face with the woman he had married thirty years ago.

His almost ex-wife Kate.

CHAPTER THREE

SHE DID THE FIRST THING she could think of: leaped back into the bathroom and slammed the door behind her. The fact that that was also the first thing a fourteen-year-old girl would do wasn't lost on her.

"Kate." His voice was low and urgent. "What the hell are you doing in there?"

"Go away," she said. "I'm trying to pretend this didn't happen."

Why did he have to have such a sexy laugh? It was only making things more difficult than they already were. "Come out or I'm coming in."

"You can't. It's a ladies' room."

"Think again. This is Paris." Land of croissants, café au lait and the unisex toilet.

She glanced behind her and saw the unmistakable porcelain evidence of its unisex capabilities. She considered climbing up onto the sink and hurling herself through the open transom window, but she was wearing a skirt.

Besides, with her luck her hips would get stuck and they'd have to call an emergency team to pry her loose and she would end up on the Parisian evening news and totally humiliate her daughters. *Mother of bride caught climbing out bathroom window of bistro.* Oh, yeah, that would make her children proud.

"Okay," she said. "You win. I'm coming out."

"This isn't a contest."

Who was he kidding? She had jumped back into the bathroom as if it were her second home. That was not what a winner would do.

"Fine," she said. "I'm coming out anyway."

She took a quick peek at the mirror, ran her fingers through her mop of curls, then pushed open the door.

The urge to jump back into the bathroom a second time was almost overwhelming, but she didn't have another token to open the door. He looked even better than he had at the engagement party four months ago and that was saying something. He had looked good enough that night for her to throw reason and self-preservation to the four winds and leap into the backseat with him. A good man in bad-boy clothing. Did it get any better than that?

Except for the divorce part it was perfect.

She reminded herself that she was forty-seven and not seventeen. She was a sophisticated, worldly woman and this was the acknowledged capital of sophisticated, worldly romantic arrangements. So what if they had a little…interlude a few months ago? This was Paris. Everyone had a little interlude now and then.

"What are you doing here?" she tossed over her shoulder as she strolled back to her table by the window.

"I was going to ask you the same thing," he said, pulling out her chair for her.

She hesitated. For all she knew he might pull the chair out from under her.

"Sit down," he said, reading her mind. "I'm too old for practical jokes."

"Better safe than sorry," she said. "I figured it might be payback." So much for sophistication. She had promised herself she would pretend the engagement party had never happened, so what did she do but be the first to bring it up.

He claimed the chair opposite her. "I'm more the water-balloon type."

He reached for his menu and she caught the glint of gold on his hand.

He's still wearing his ring....

She ran a nervous hand through her tangle of curls, aware of her own naked ring finger. "Never mention water balloons around a woman with frizzy hair."

"Your hair looks great."

"I haven't combed it since somewhere over the Atlantic."

"Don't do this, Kate."

"Do what?"

"You know what."

"If I knew what, I wouldn't ask what."

"You're doing it again."

"I know. I can't help it."

"You never could take a compliment."

"Not much practice."

He winced. So did she. This wasn't going well at all.

"Let's start over," she said as Ryan gestured for the server. "How about we limit conversation to the weather, the food and the wedding."

Again that twinkle in his eye, the one that always got them into trouble. "That should see us through lunch," Ryan said.

"You're ordering lunch?"

He nodded. "Your soup looks great."

"It is great," she admitted, "but what I really want is a plateful of pastries and a huge café au lait."

"So order it."

"This soup must be a thousand calories in cheese alone."

He shrugged his shoulders. "You're in Paris."

"And I brought my American thighs with me."

"Your thighs are the same as they were in high school."

"That's a nasty thing to say."

"You really do need to work on this compliment thing, Kate."

She started to repeat her *not enough practice* remark from earlier on, but something stopped her. *The truth, maybe?* He had never held back on compliments. She had simply stopped hearing them.

The server, a petite blonde named Chloe, appeared at their table. Kate laughed as he searched around for the French words for "onion soup" then settled for pointing at her bowl and her glass of wine.

"Of course," Chloe said in perfect English. "I'll be right back."

They locked eyes and started to laugh.

"Give it up," Kate said. "Everyone here speaks better English than we do."

"I didn't come to Paris to practice my English," he said in mock annoyance.

Chloe returned with his soup and wine. Kate ordered a café au lait and an assortment of buttery glazed goodies.

"Make that for two," Ryan said.

"Café au lait?" Kate raised a brow. "Since when?"

"Since they opened a fancy coffee shop around the corner from the radio station." He spooned up some soup. "Since when do you drink red wine?"

"Since about thirty minutes ago." She wrinkled her nose. "Turns out I still don't like it."

"Big surprise. It didn't come with a paper umbrella and pineapple spear."

She laughed again. "So I'm not an oenophile. Sue me."

"Remember the year we went to that wine tasting in Pennsylvania?"

"Oh God!" She pretended to hide her face behind her hands. "I've spent fifteen years trying to forget that weekend."

Her parents had volunteered to take care of the girls so they could spend four days in Lancaster County to celebrate their anniversary. The waitress in the pancake place told them about a tiny local winery that hosted tastings on the weekend. Kate, who never drank anything that didn't come with paper parasols, pineapple spears and bright red maraschino cherries, found herself enamored of something called Holiday Wine that tasted like a blend of toothpaste, cloves and red hots.

The hangover lasted a full day.

"Remember the room we had?"

Of course she remembered. That tiny room was all bed. A big fluffy inviting bed made for lovers. The kind of bed a woman never forgot.

She shifted position in her chair. "Your soup's getting cold."

"My soup's fine."

"The melted cheese gets all rubbery. You really should—"

"The kids are grown, Kate, and I'm almost forty-eight. You can relax. We can all feed ourselves."

"Fine," she said, polishing off the last drops of red wine in her glass. "Whatever."

"I didn't mean it that way."

"I know that."

She wasn't sure she did and, from the look in his eyes, he wasn't all that sure, either.

"You worry too much, that's all."

"You mean, I'm too controlling," she said.

"I didn't say that."

"No, but that's what you meant."

"No," he corrected her, "I said exactly what I meant. You worry too much. You always have. Don't read more into it."

"I have an idea," she said, after Chloe replaced her soup and wine with butter, starch and caffeine. "We have a long week ahead of us. Why don't we put a lid on the past and keep things light?"

His expression was anything but. "Meaning what?"

Did he really want her to spell it out? "I don't want to walk down memory lane with you, Ryan. There's no point to it. We've had good times and not-so-good ones over the years, but that's over. I don't want to think about any of it."

"You're talking about what happened at the engagement party."

"I'm talking about everything. Two weeks from now we'll be officially divorced. I think we've said everything that needs to be said, don't you?"

He took a long sip of wine. "There's nothing wrong with sharing memories."

"We'll be sharing plenty of them with the family once we both arrive at Milles Fleurs."

He leaned back in his chair. "You're right," he said. "We'll keep the chat to onion soup and the fact that there's a rottweiler sitting at the next table eating foie gras from a spoon."

She spun around so fast she almost fell off her chair. He wasn't kidding. A giant dog was happily lapping goose liver from a spoon while his owner— or lunch date—sipped wine and read a book.

"I guess we're not in Kansas anymore," she muttered as she swiveled back to face Ryan.

"Or New York," he said.

She met his eyes. "Or Boston, for that matter."

"Don't be so sure about Boston," he said, a slight smile playing at the corners of his mouth. "I saw a Jack Russell order a Guinness a few weeks ago."

She wanted to laugh, but an emotion she didn't dare name threatened to overwhelm her. "I stand corrected."

"We did it, Katie," he said.

She wasn't going to pretend she didn't understand.

"I guess we did," she admitted, "although this isn't quite the way we thought it would be."

Too much information. Aren't you the one who wanted to keep it light?

He lifted his half-empty glass of red wine. "To Paris."

She lifted her café au lait. "To Paris."

Now all she had to do was get through lunch without a meltdown and she would be home-free.

CHAPTER FOUR

MAYBE IT WAS THE COFFEE.

Maybe it was the gigantic butter-and-sugar rush from the sinfully delectable platter of pastries they demolished between them.

Whatever the reason, both Kate and Ryan were feeling exceptionally mellow as they left the bistro.

"It's like a street fair out here," Ryan said as they dodged a platoon of roller skaters whizzing by. A violinist played a mournful tune on the corner while a young girl countered with every tourist's favorite French music cliché *La Vie en Rose* on an accordion on the opposite corner. Couples strolled by hand in hand. Businessmen and -women talked swiftly into cell phones as they hurried to their next appointments. An elderly couple cuddled together on a bench alongside the river, letting the day flow all around them.

Life was happening everywhere they looked.

Kate rummaged in her purse for her sunglasses. "Lunch was great," she said, slipping the sunglasses on. "Thanks."

He inclined his head. "Thanks for letting me join you."

"I never did like eating alone."

Oops. Not exactly what she meant to say. She hoped the red wine he'd polished off at lunch had taken the edge off his powers of perception.

"So where are you headed?" He sounded surprisingly unsure of himself. She wished she didn't find that so endearing. The man she had spent most of her life with had seemed so sure of everything.

"The Eiffel Tower," she said with a slightly embarrassed laugh. "Where else would an American tourist on her first trip to Paris go?"

He laughed with her and she hesitated. Should she ask if he wanted to walk along with her or was he looking for a graceful way to say goodbye?

"Well," she said, starting to inch slowly away, "I guess I'll see you at the inn."

"The Eiffel Tower is number one on my American-tourist-in-Paris list, too," he said. "Mind if I walk with you?"

Talk about a loaded question. If she told the truth, she would look like she was carrying a torch for him. If she told a lie, her first day in Paris would lose most of its luster.

"Fair warning," she said in what she hoped was a breezy, I-don't-care tone of voice. "I have a camera and I'm not afraid to use it."

He reached into the back pocket of his jeans. "And I have my guidebook."

Why fight fate? The sun was shining. The breeze was sweet with spring. And this was Paris.

They crossed the street and walked along the Seine in the general direction of the Eiffel Tower. The city surged with creative energy. In many ways it reminded her of New York. She was about to say that to Ryan when he stopped short.

"Hey! Isn't that Alexis coming out of the salon across the street?"

She looked, squinted, raised her sunglasses then let out a muffled shriek. "I'm not here," she said, then took off as fast as two café au laits and three cream-filled pastries would let her.

WHAT THE HELL—?

He blinked as she disappeared down the narrow alley between the *boulangerie* and *magasin de fleur.* The last time she had taken off like that was the night of the engagement party. He had let her go that time and lived to regret it. This time she wasn't going to get away so easily.

His daughter was busy laughing with a group of young women in front of the salon across the street. She hadn't a clue her estranged parents were performing a little bit of street theater one hundred yards away. He darted down the alleyway before she had the chance to find out.

"What the hell are you doing?" he demanded when he caught up to a gasping Kate halfway between the street and the river. "You're not running off on me again without an explanation."

Kate was bent over at the waist, gasping for air. "I need oxygen," she managed. "I'm too old for all this drama."

"You're not smoking again, are you?"

"I'm not running, either. I'm out of shape."

"You probably weigh the same as you did in high school."

"Yes, but it's all in different places."

"I like the different places." That wasn't what he had meant to say. He had meant to ask why the hell she had turned into The Fugitive when he pointed out their daughter across the street.

She looked up at him, blue eyes wide. "Ryan, I—"

He touched the tip of his finger to the corner of her mouth. "Sugar," he said.

Her tongue darted out to capture the sweetness. An involuntary act, but the effect it had on him was powerful.

He ducked his head and caught the familiar smell of her hair. She leaned closer, all softness and warmth.

"We're in Paris," he whispered against her lips and she whispered back, "We're in Paris."

And then he kissed her.

THE KISS WAS MORE PROMISE than fact. A quick brush of his mouth to hers. Not tentative but testing. As if he expected her to turn and run away again.

Which was exactly what she should do. This was worse than playing with fire. Was the magic of Paris enough to make up for the fact that this could be the fast track to disaster just days before their daughter's wedding?

A smarter woman would have taken a step back, but then maybe she wasn't as bright as she thought.

All she cared about was the strange and familiar feel of his mouth on hers, the smell of his skin, the muscled hardness of his chest as they melted together in an embrace.

"Now I know I'm really in Paris," she said, ending the kiss before it went too far. "Making out in an alleyway with a good-looking guy."

Her attempt at humor didn't knock him off track the way she hoped it would.

"Why did you run?"

"I run all the time," she said lightly. "To the store. To the studio. To the corner bakery. You'll have to be more specific."

"Just now," he said. "From Alexis. You didn't want her to see us together, did you?"

"I didn't want her to see me, period. The girls think I'm off meeting a client. They're not expecting me for another two days." She withheld the part about Celeste and Paris and memories of their younger selves. "Sounds ridiculous, doesn't it?"

He grinned. "They don't know I'm in town, either."

"You're kidding." She started to laugh. "They really don't know you're here?"

"I was in London interviewing a soccer player. It was supposed to take a few days, but he wasn't exactly verbal. We finished in an hour so—" he shrugged "—here I am."

"She didn't see me, did she?"

"Taylor was there, too. I managed to duck out before they crossed the street."

They locked eyes and burst into laughter.

"The last time I took off like that, I was ten and I'd lobbed a baseball through Mr. Maguire's front window," Ryan said.

"I won't blow your cover if you don't blow mine."

"We were always good at keeping each other's secrets."

"And there were so many of them." She gestured toward the street. "Do you think it's safe?"

"We can't stay in this alleyway all day."

"Good point."

"Stay behind me. I'll cover you while we check it out."

It was so absurd that they had to laugh, and once they started they found it impossible to stop. Kate leaned against the wall, crying from laughter, while Ryan made a three-act production of poking his head out and looking up and down the street.

If you have so much fun with the man, why are you divorcing him?

Because life wasn't all stealing kisses in a Parisian alleyway, that was why. You could love somebody, enjoy his company and still not be able to make it work for the long haul.

Wasn't that the reason they had given each other when they agreed to part? Funny how it didn't sound quite so logical right now.

"All clear," he said, wiping imaginary sweat from his brow. "Not a Donovan in sight."

They joined the street traffic and started walking toward the Eiffel Tower once again.

"I never thought I'd be ducking my own kids on my first trip to Paris," Kate said as they waited for the traffic signal to change. "Life is nothing if not surprising."

He stopped and pointed toward a knot of young women posing for photos alongside the river. "Isn't that Alexis over there?"

Kate turned to run, but he stopped her.

"Gotcha!"

"Not funny."

"So why are you laughing?"

"Because I happen to be a sucker for really terrible jokes."

"Ouch."

It was her turn to grin. "Gotcha!"

They bantered back and forth as they walked, then settled into companionable silence, breathing the air, taking in the sights, reveling in the fact that they were walking the streets of the most beautiful city on the planet.

"Look at that line!" Kate said when they neared the Eiffel Tower. "That's worse than the Pirates of the Caribbean ride the time we took the girls to Disney World."

"I say we ditch it."

"I agree." She would come back tomorrow morning when it opened.

"Now what?" He whipped out his guidebook. "The Louvre is over that way."

"The Louvre?" She arched a brow. "I find it hard to believe that's your number-one choice."

"It wasn't." He pointed at the Eiffel Tower. "That was. Remember?"

"The Louvre will take hours. Maybe we should just—"

He grabbed her hand for the second time. "Come on!"

They ducked into a pastry shop with seconds to spare. Alexis and her sister and two other members of the wedding party strolled past the window, laughing and looking impossibly young and beautiful.

"Somebody had better tell that girl she has a

wedding to prepare for," Kate muttered. "She has too much time on her hands."

Ryan, who was checking out a bouquet of warm baguettes fresh from the oven, laughed.

Kate stifled a yawn as Ryan picked a small baguette and handed over some coinage. He broke off a piece of soft, warm bread and handed it to her.

"Heavenly," she said with a sigh. Once again they stepped out onto the busy street and started walking. "I'm not even hungry, but I can't resist." So far the French baked goods she had sampled were a few rungs above heavenly. She yawned again. "I hate to say this, but I don't think I'm up for the Louvre."

"Jet lag?"

"That and the fact I haven't slept for two days. I'm going to go back to my hotel and crash until dinner." She gave his arm a quick friendly squeeze. "See you at Milles Fleurs."

It would have been the perfect exit line if he hadn't fallen into step beside her.

"What are you doing?"

"I'm walking you back."

"You don't know where I'm staying."

"I'll find out when we get there."

"You really don't have to do this. I can find my way."

"I know you can," he said. "I thought we could talk about the wedding."

"I know as much about it as you do. Alexis said it was all going to be a surprise and the only thing I had to do was show up with my dress and shoes. She would do the rest."

"She told me the same thing."

"To bring your dress and shoes?"

He pretended to glare at her. "The male equivalent."

"I'm not so sure our girl will be moving back stateside, are you?"

He shook his head. "Not sure at all. I think she's more like Aunt Celeste than anyone else in the family."

"I was thinking the same thing."

"How will you feel if she decides to make her home in France?"

"Sad," Kate said. "Happy that she's following her heart but sad that we won't get to see her very often."

"She'll only be a plane ride away," Ryan pointed out.

"There's a big difference between a transatlantic flight and the shuttle to Boston." She *would* pick Boston. "Or D.C.," she added in a lame attempt to cover up. "You know what I mean."

"I do know," he said. "Sometimes Boston feels like the other side of the planet to me."

His words hit her hard. His big move to Boston two years ago had been a huge success career-wise but was it possible he still had some regrets?

Then again what difference did it make? His regrets were his business, not hers. In ten days they would sign the papers and their divorce would be official. It wouldn't hurt her to keep reminding herself of that fact every thirty seconds or so.

HE HAD PUT IT OUT there like a trial balloon, but so far she hadn't picked up on it. The old Kate would have been all over that statement with a microscope, but the new Kate just smiled and continued walking in the direction of her hotel.

She had him completely off balance. The kiss they had shared in the alleyway had been filled with heat and promise, but you would never know it from the cool and distant friendliness she displayed now.

Maybe he was the one with the microscope this time, examining every smile, every word for—

For what? Now that was the question of the hour. What the hell was the point? It was over. All he had to do was look at the way she wasn't looking at him to know she had moved on, leaving him and everything they had shared behind.

I made a mistake, Kate. I should have listened to what you were saying. I should have understood what you needed. We could have found a way to make it work...a compromise...maybe even one of those commuter marriages if that was the only way....

It took him a second to realize she had stopped walking.

It took him another second to realize they were standing in front of the Hotel St. Michel.

"What's up?" he asked. "Another daughter sighting?"

She shook her head. "This is my stop," she said, tilting her head toward the entrance.

"You're staying here?"

"Yes." She looked up at him. "Why are you looking at me like that?"

"I'm staying here, too."

"This place isn't even in the guidebooks. The only way you could possibly know about it is if Aunt Celeste—"

She stopped.

They locked eyes.

She pulled the key to Room 625 from her bag.

He pulled the key to Room 625 from his back pocket.

"Houston," she said, "we have a problem."

CHAPTER FIVE

"CELESTE," Kate said as they rode the elevator up to the sixth floor. "She set us up."

"She wouldn't do that," Ryan said, as the elevator doors slid open and they exited into the hallway. "She's almost ninety. She must have made a mistake."

"This isn't a mistake. Aunt Celeste knew exactly what she was doing."

Her great-aunt was a born matchmaker who had tried to set up the undertaker with the hospice nurse at her husband's funeral.

"She wouldn't do that."

"Oh yes, she would," Kate said, "and I'll prove it."

The elevator doors slid open and they exited into the hallway.

"Okay, here's a question. Did Aunt Celeste have anything to do with that interview you did in London?"

The look of disbelief on Ryan's face was starting to be replaced by one of shock. "She put me in touch with the footballer."

"I rest my case." She couldn't keep the smug note of triumph from her voice. "This was a setup."

"The guy announced his retirement to me. I don't think your Aunt Celeste had anything to do with that."

"Don't bet on it," Kate said. "When it comes to romance, she's Patton in pearls. Nothing gets in her way."

"Let's not jump to conclusions. Maybe the desk clerk gave me the wrong key by accident."

"Right," said Kate as she slid the old-fashioned brass key into the lock and opened the door. "And I suppose your bags were put here by accident, too."

A familiar leather carry-on and a duffel bag had been left in the hallway adjacent to the escritoire.

"Believe me now?" she asked.

He dragged his hand through his hair and whistled low. "I didn't think she had it in her."

"That's because you're a man. She can work right there in plain sight and you'd never see it coming."

"Hey, Nancy Drew, you didn't see it coming, either."

She stalked across the room and picked up the phone.

"What are you doing?" He had the look of a man who had been dropped behind enemy lines without a battle plan.

"I'm calling Celeste. I want you to hear it from her own lips."

The phone rang twice at the inn. A woman answered with a cheery *"'Allo!"*

Kate, cheeks flaming with embarrassment, stumbled through a mixed-up mess of English and high-school French as she tried to get the woman to take the phone to her aunt.

"Non! Non!" This was followed by a stream of rapid-fire French that made Kate dizzy.

"Madame Beaulieu, s'il vous plaît," she tried again. *"Je m'appelle Kate Donovan. Je suis sa niece."*

"Madame Beaulieu away…"

Kate thanked the woman and hung up. She turned to Ryan. "The inn says she's not there." She then said something she would have punished her daughters for saying when they were ten years old.

He had been her husband long enough not to laugh.

"You think she's ducking your call?"

"What else?" She handed him the phone. "You call and say there's a wedding emergency."

"Like hell. I like Celeste."

"Do you like what she did to us?"

Wait a minute! What if he did like what Celeste did? Wouldn't that be something.

He took the phone from her and dialed 0, which effectively brought that line of conjecture to a halt.

"Je m'appelle Ryan Donovan in six twenty-

five. There's been…*une erreur.*" He covered the mouthpiece with his hand. "How do you say 'change my room' in French?"

She scrambled through her carry-on for her French-to-English dictionary. "*Chambre* is room," she offered, flipping through the pages. "Try *une chambre autre* with a question mark in your voice and see what happens."

He shot her a "fat lot of good that's gonna do me" kind of look.

"It doesn't matter," he said into the phone. "*Une petit…un autre chambre s'il vous plaît.*" He looked over at Kate. "He put me on hold."

"Hang up."

He didn't.

"Hang up," she said again then wrestled the phone from his hand just as the clerk came back on line. "*Merci,*" she said, "but *ma chambre est parfait…bien…au revoir.*" God only knows what she had really said to the desk clerk but it seemed to have worked.

Ryan, however, was less than thrilled.

"Now how the hell am I going to get another room?"

"Thanks to Celeste, you already have a room. We're not children. We should be able to make the best of this situation." *I don't want you to leave, Ryan. This is the best thing Aunt Celeste ever did for me.*

"There must be thousands of rooms out there. I'm going to—" He yawned behind his hand. "Sorry."

"That's okay." She stifled her own yawn. "I haven't slept in two days."

"Make it one and a half," he said, yawning again.

"I'm too tired to argue. Why don't you at least grab a nap before you go looking for a room," she suggested, hoping she sounded more nonchalant than she felt. "You're out on your feet."

"So are you," he said. "You look wiped out."

"You take the sofa," she said. "I'll dig up a pillow for you."

She couldn't help but notice that he didn't seem at all unhappy with the suggestion. She also couldn't help but notice her own delight. Maybe she was more like her aunt than she had ever realized.

"Skip the pillow. I'm so tired I could sleep standing up."

"There's only the one bathroom," she said, pointing to the doorway beyond the bedroom. "If you'd like to use it first …"

"Thanks." He disappeared into the other room.

If she wasn't so hideously tired, she would be proud of them for being so adult and pragmatic about the situation, but the truth was the whole thing suddenly made her terribly sad. They had lived together as husband and wife for almost thirty years and here they were as stiff and formal as strangers on a train.

They hadn't lived together for almost two years. They were the blink of an eye away from signing final divorce papers. You would think she would be used to the idea by now, but she wasn't. Their secret lovemaking on the night of the engagement party had reawakened feelings she had believed dead and buried, and seeing him today hurt more than she cared to admit.

She liked seeing the light glowing under the bathroom door. She liked the sound of him belting out Motown oldies in the shower even if he was the world's worst singer. She liked the shoes in the hallway, the comb and wallet and keys on top of the nightstand. It all felt so familiar, so right, so dangerous.

That was the word for it. *Dangerous.* He was seeing someone else. Some unnamed twinkie who worked at the station and whose only goal in life was to rock his world. Though why her children thought she needed that piece of information was beyond her.

They had had plenty of time to work things out and it hadn't happened. Look at the incident in the rented Toyota. He could have run after her when she leaped from the car. He could have followed her into the house and tried to make sense out of what had happened. But he didn't do anything and, to be fair, neither did she. The weeks and the months rolled on as they let their lawyers and their daughters do their talking for them.

And now there she was, sitting on the edge of Aunt Celeste's lovely sofa in the middle of Aunt Celeste's lovely suite of rooms in painfully lovely Paris, listening to her husband take a shower. She hadn't been this happy since that night in the rented Toyota when she went temporarily insane.

RYAN STOOD naked in the middle of the luxuriously appointed bathroom and considered the problem.

His clean clothes were in his bag in the hallway, which wouldn't be a big deal if Kate weren't out there waiting to claim the bathroom for herself.

What the hell was the right thing to do? It wasn't that they hadn't seen each other naked thousands of times over the years. They knew each other's bodies intimately. Every sweet curve, every slender—

Hold on, pal. This is about your body, not hers.

He regrouped. In another time and place, he wouldn't have thought twice about walking naked from point A to point B. But those days were long gone. He wasn't in bad shape for his age but—

Scratch naked.

He was surprised there wasn't a terry-cloth robe hanging behind the door. That would have made life a hell of a lot easier. So that left the towel. Unfortunately it wasn't a big towel. Just your average bath towel, the kind you had to hang on to to keep it in place.

Hey, fool, it isn't brain surgery. All he had to do was stroll nonchalantly through the bedroom, the sitting room, grab his bag from the foyer, then reverse the process with Kate watching every move.

She was an artist. She noticed everything. Those sharp eyes would zero in on the inevitable signs of age, but he knew that her compassionate heart would look the other way.

He was starting to understand why she had fled from him the night of Alexis's engagement party. Sometimes running was the only option.

He tugged the towel around his middle and held it with a death grip.

Time to face the music.

A STOLEN MOMENT in the backseat of a car was one thing.

Watching a man cross the room wearing nothing but a towel was something else again.

He was beautiful. So beautiful it took all of her self-control to keep from grabbing a sketch pad and vine of charcoal and capturing him before the image vanished. She was trained in the architecture of the human form. She had put in her time at life classes. It was all angle and curve, light and shadow.

She had seen more perfect bodies, faces so exquisitely balanced they stole your breath away. But none of those perfect bodies or heavenly faces had ever made her heart feel like breaking the way it did right now as Ryan walked past her into the hallway to get his bag.

"Sorry," she said as he made his way back toward the bathroom. "I should've realized you'd need your stuff."

"No problem," he said. "I don't expect you to pick up the slack for me."

Was he telling her he didn't need her or was he saying he didn't expect maid service from his estranged wife? She wasn't sure.

He stopped in the doorway. "I didn't mean that the way it sounded."

"I know that."

She scrupulously maintained eye contact, not letting her gaze move down over his broad chest, and still-flat stomach, and—

Full stop.

"I'll be out in a minute," he said. "You look like you're ready to crash."

"Take your time," she managed. "I'm fine."

Although if he wanted to stand in the doorway in that towel for an hour or two, she wouldn't complain.

He touched her heart. He had from the first moment they met a hundred years ago. Nothing had changed that fact. Not time. Not distance.

And probably not even divorce.

HE WAS ASLEEP by the time she washed her face and brushed her teeth.

She slipped out of the bathroom in a T-shirt and a pair of silky drawstring pants and padded softly to the archway that separated the bedroom from the sitting room. He was sprawled on the sofa with his back to her. She smiled to herself at the sight of his bare feet propped on the armrest. In all the years they had been together, they had never found a sofa he could stretch out on without making an accommodation.

He shifted position and she ducked back into the bedroom, feeling strangely guilty and more than a little aroused.

Well, too bad for you, she thought as she slid under the duvet. What was it her mother used to say about making your own bed? Clearly she had not only made her bed, now she was lying in it.

Alone.

CHAPTER SIX

RYAN COULDN'T SLEEP.

It wasn't the couch's fault. Or the fault of the bright late-afternoon sun streaming through the windows or the ancient creak of the elevator as it ferried guests between floors.

He couldn't sleep because the only woman he had ever loved was curled up in bed not twenty feet away from him and it might as well have been twenty miles.

He had sensed her watching him from the doorway. You didn't love a woman for as long as you could remember and not know when she was watching you. He heard the familiar sound of her footsteps as she stepped back into the bedroom, the silken rustle as she slid between the sheets, her soft rhythmic breathing when she finally drifted off to sleep.

It would have been an easy thing to climb into that bed with her. To sleep next to her one more time, wake up with her in his arms and slip away before she awoke. His wife had slept through hurricanes. She would never have known.

Which was one big reason he stayed on the sofa. He wanted her to know. He wanted her to want him there next to her. Anything less was second best.

They had slept together every night for almost three decades. She would curl into him, her bottom against his groin, soft breasts warm against his arm, and he would listen to the rhythm of her breathing as it grew slower, more regular, and she dropped into sleep. Deep in the heart of the night he felt closer to her than he did during the day, more sure of his place in her heart.

Had he ever told her that? He couldn't remember. They had been thrown into the deep end of the pool right from the start. Pregnant, married, and barely eighteen years old—the odds had been against them, but somehow they had loved each other enough to make it work for a very long time.

They had survived three kids in seven years, more trips to the E.R. than either one of them could count, money problems, job stresses, changing priorities, answered prayers and then suddenly when it seemed like they had left the tough stuff behind and it would be smooth sailing from hereon out they fell apart.

And he hadn't even seen it coming.

Maybe he should have. Maybe she had been sending him signals for years and he hadn't been paying attention.

If he had a dollar for every *maybe* he could score them a suite at the Plaza Athenee for a year and have money left over to send his future grand-kids to Harvard.

He wanted her. He wanted to feel her soft body against him, breathe in the smell of her hair, her skin, her breath. He wanted to make love to her, every inch, every secret place, until the separation, the upcoming divorce, all of it fell away and it was just the two of them alone with their dream of Paris.

But that wasn't the way life worked.

He lay on the couch while his wife slept sweetly in the other room, and he listened to the sound of an ancient elevator creaking its way past the sixth floor until, exhausted, he finally slept, too.

A SURPRISE VISIT from Helene, their chambermaid, startled them both awake a little after six o'clock. Helene didn't speak much English so they communicated through an amalgam of French, English and hand gestures as she bustled about the suite, fluffing pillows, swapping damp towels for dry fluffy ones, and doing anything else that needed doing.

"What's her problem?" Ryan asked as the door closed behind the maid. "She looked pissed off."

"She's accustomed to Celeste," Kate said after the woman left. "I think we're too self-sufficient for her taste."

Ryan looked sleepy and rumpled. She was very partial to sleepy, rumpled men.

"I'd better push off," he said, combing his hair with his fingers. "I need to find a place to stay."

It was now or never.

"I think you should stay here."

He looked as surprised as she was by her words. "You're playing right into Celeste's hands, you know that. If what you say is true, that's exactly what she wants."

"It's a beautiful suite," she said, refusing to heed the alarm bells going off inside her head, "and we're two mature adults. If you don't mind the couch…"

He studied her for what seemed like forever. "The couch is fine. If you don't mind the company."

"There's safety in numbers. Between the two of us, we should be able to duck our daughters until we get to Milles Fleurs."

Lame, Kate. Why don't you try something subtle, like throwing yourself into his arms?

"I don't know about you," he said, "but I can't wait until ten or eleven o'clock to eat dinner. I'm on American time."

She let out a huge theatrical sigh of relief. "I'm so hungry I'd brave an early-bird special."

"Get dressed," he said. "We're in Paris. Let's not waste it."

SHE LOOKED like a girl as she dashed off to the bedroom to dress for dinner. Her curly auburn hair was soft and loose around her face. Her body, slender but curvy, was clearly visible through the thin T-shirt and silky pants. Thirty years and three children later and she was as beautiful to him now as she had been at the start.

He wasn't blind to the changes the years had brought with them. The faint lines at the outer corners of her eyes. The narrow white streak over her left temple. The sadness behind the easy smile. They had been through so much together. She had held him tight when he lost his parents. He had been there for her when her mother fought a losing battle with cancer. Nobody on earth knew him the way she did. Nobody else ever would.

In a few days they would gather with family and friends to celebrate their daughter's wedding. A few days after that they would show up at their respective lawyers' offices and sign the papers that officially ended their marriage.

How the hell had it gone this far?

He had never met a problem he couldn't solve, a wall he couldn't break through. When he set his sights on a goal, it was as good as done.

Except with Kate.

There had always been a tiny part of Kate, a spark of something indefinable, that he had never been able to capture long enough to understand. He dealt with raw power and muscle, batting averages and earned-run averages, pass-rush averages and turnovers and receptions. Tangible things you could count up in neat rows and keep track of on a graph or pie chart.

Kate was quicksilver in his hands. There was nothing calculated about her, no artifice at all, but somehow she managed to keep him slightly off balance in ways he couldn't predict or defend himself against. She had been the most dependable wife and mother on the planet and still he had found himself waiting for her to wake up one morning and say, "This was fun but I'm out of here," and take up the life of an artist.

Which in many ways was exactly what had happened when he took the job in Boston.

He should never have let her go.

THEY FOUND a cozy little brasserie around the corner from the Plaza Athenee that the guidebooks all claimed made the best roast chicken with rosemary on the planet. A pair of chunky ivory candles glowed softly on the table. The Beaujolais shimmered like rubies in the heavy wine goblets. Music, unfamiliar but wonderful, floated toward them from some unseen source. A Cavalier King Charles spaniel slept at the feet of his owner at the table near the door.

"The eavesdropping would be great here," Ryan said, "if I could understand a word they were saying."

"I was thinking the same thing," Kate said with a laugh. "That couple over there—the ones with the baby asleep between them? You can tell they're talking about something serious, but so far the only words I've been able to make out are *chicken* and *butterfat*."

"A serious discussion about chicken and butterfat?"

She pretended to be insulted. "Hey, I only translate. I don't analyze."

They kept up the banter over a seriously delicious dinner of golden roast chicken, crisp *pommes frites,* and a frisée salad garnished with cornichons. The wine flowed freely and to their surprise so did the conversation.

He told her stories about the radio station where he worked, the crazy callers, the pressure to grow the ratings, adjusting to the rhythm of a different city.

I miss you, Katie. I miss our home, I miss New York, I miss the life we had together.

She told him about the leap her career had taken. She told him about the new portrait commissions, the small write-up in next month's *Art Journal*.

I must have been crazy. I can paint anywhere on the planet. Why did I let you leave that way? she thought.

He toasted her latest commission.

Are you in love with someone else, Katie? Am I too late?

She toasted his latest market share.

The girls worry that you might have found someone else, Ryan. Don't you ever wonder if we're making a big mistake?

Maybe it was the wine. Maybe it was the fact that she had nothing to lose. But she decided to throw caution to the wind.

"The girls told me you're seeing someone."

"The girls are wrong."

"They said she's a producer at your radio station."

"Ellen?" He started to laugh. "We're friends. She's married with three kids."

"So are you." Great. Another *oops* moment for the memory book.

"I'm not seeing anyone, Kate." He leveled her with a look. "What about you? Taylor said you went out to dinner with some Wall Street type you met at a gallery."

"I did." She paused for effect, liking the look of pained curiosity in his eyes. "He told me it was time I thought about planning for retirement. He actually deducted the cost of our dinner on his taxes."

God, she loved his laugh. Maybe if they had taken more time to laugh in the past few years they would still be together.

"Looks like our girls were trying to stir things up a little."

"I guess it comes with the territory."

"For the record, there hasn't been anyone since you, Kate."

She met his eyes across the table. "I don't know what to say."

"Don't say anything. I wanted you to know."

She nodded. It shouldn't matter to her but it did. "I've been concentrating on my painting. I haven't had time for anything else." Was that relief she saw in his eyes? She hoped so.

"Things are good?"

"Things are good. I have more commissions than I know what to do with." She knocked twice on the tabletop. "I think I'm finally on the right track." She had finally stopped painting from her head and started painting from her heart and from that moment on her fortunes changed.

"And Manhattan puts you right in the middle of the art world."

"Good for business, bad for work," she said, polishing off the last of her wine. "I find myself driving out to the house whenever I want to settle down and concentrate."

"I thought every artist dreamed about setting up a studio in a SoHo loft."

"Be careful what you wish for," she said, throwing caution to the wind. "Turns out I do my best work on our old back porch. I don't think I'll renew the sublet."

"I miss writing my old newspaper column," he said. "The radio call-in show is fun but I'm just the ringmaster."

"Why can't you do both?"

"Because I don't have you."

It wasn't the answer she had expected and she looked down at her empty dinner plate. It was the answer she had been praying for without realizing it for two years.

"Don't say anything," he told her. "Just listen."

He said things she had never heard before. At least she hadn't heard them the way she was hearing them tonight, with her heart wide-open. It wasn't that he hadn't told her a thousand times how much he loved her, how much he valued who she was and what she brought to his life. Somewhere along the way she had stopped listening, but she was listening now, letting the words slide past her defenses and find their mark.

The server wheeled over the pastry cart and they went a little crazy, choosing one of just about everything. They ate and they talked. They sipped after-dinner cordials and talked some more.

She heard herself telling him about her painting and realized it had been years since she had opened up to him this way.

"This is the age of photography," he said, as they held hands beneath the table. "Why do people still sit for portraits?"

She launched into an art-school explanation of tradition and cultural expectations within certain economic demographics then laughed when he pretended to fall asleep with his face in the cheese platter.

"From the heart," he said. "Why do they want what you can give them?"

She had taken dozens of classes, sat through scores of workshops while he watched the kids. She had let him see the brushes and the paints and the canvases but she had never once let him into the heart of it.

"Because sometimes it's magic," she said at last. "People change when they sit for a portrait. When the chemistry is right, a portrait not only captures the subject's physical self, it reveals her heart and soul and maybe the artist's as well. Cameras can capture what was, but it takes the prism of an artist's creativity to see what might be.

"I know how crazy it sounds," she said when she paused to take a breath, "but you asked."

"I've asked before," he pointed out gently, "but this is the first time you ever really answered."

"Too much information?"

He shook his head. "Not even close."

By the time they reached the dessert course, they were both pleasantly looped. The cordial served with coffee didn't help matters. Neither did the delicious rum-soaked cake.

"Do you think they'd mind if we spent the night here?" Kate asked as she finished the last of the cake. "I'd like to curl up and take a nap."

"Good thing we didn't come by car," Ryan said. "We'd need to hire a designated driver."

"I'm not drunk," she protested. "Just very relaxed."

"Don't try to walk a straight line when you say that."

They floated out of the restaurant on a cloud of great food, great conversation and great cognac. Kate thought she saw her brother and his wife walking toward them and she yanked Ryan into an alcove until the coast was clear. Ryan was sure Alexis and Gabe waved at them from the window of a passing cab. He twirled her behind a lamppost.

They felt lighthearted, silly, deliriously and unexpectedly happy.

Linking arms as they walked the cobbled street seemed the natural thing to do.

"There are more Donovans here than back in New York," Ryan observed. "Who's watching the city?"

This struck Kate as hilariously funny.

"Yep," said Ryan. "You definitely had too much brandy."

Which was probably true, but who cared? She hadn't been this happy in years.

"Oh, look," Kate said. "I see old Mr. Gardner from the hardware store." She pretended to hide behind Ryan, who ducked his head and pulled up the collar of his shirt to shield his identity.

Seconds later he grabbed her hand and started running toward the Eiffel Tower.

"I'm in heels," Kate protested, "and I've had way too much cognac. Why are we running?"

"Remember Mrs. Harmel?"

She thought for a second. "Our home-room teacher?"

"She waved at us from the window of that bistro over there."

She couldn't help it. She started laughing all over again. They saw the kid who used to deliver their daily paper twenty years ago. They saw her Uncle Bob from New Jersey who was eighty-seven and determined to die without ever once setting foot outside the Garden State. They saw Santa Claus, Easter Bunny, and an assortment of cousins, high-school classmates and Mick Jagger.

By the time they reached the base of the Eiffel Tower they had laughed so hard and so long, their sides ached.

"What if one of our clan really did see us together?" Kate asked as they leaned against a railing and tried to catch their breath.

He shrugged. "If they did, they did."

"How would we explain this?"

"We'd tell them it was none of their business."

"We couldn't do that."

"Why not? It *isn't* any of their business."

"I know. But they're family. They—"

Her words caught in her throat. The sky was the color of spilled India ink, spangled with stars. The sight of the Eiffel Tower soaring up into the darkness, glowing like a column of diamonds, made her shiver.

He drew her into his arms and she rested her head against his shoulder and let it all wash over her. The sweetness. The wonder. The pain. She couldn't escape any of it, and for once she didn't want to.

For a little while they were just another pair of lovers lost in their own world. Nobody gave them a second glance. This was Paris, after all, and it was only a matter of time.

THEY WERE QUIET as they walked back to the hotel. Something had changed between them. She couldn't see it or hear it, but she knew it just the same.

They were moving toward each other across time and space and nothing short of a meteor strike could knock them off course.

They nodded to the doorman as they crossed the lobby of the Hotel St. Michel. They nodded to the desk clerk as they walked toward the elevator. They made polite conversation with the elevator operator as they creaked and rattled up to the sixth floor.

They fell silent as Ryan turned the key in the lock and opened the door to Room 625.

Small lamps burned in the entrance hall and in the sitting room, casting a soft pink glow. A bottle of brandy and two snifters rested on a tray atop a side table next to a small vase of perfect ivory roses. The sheer curtains at the windows billowed in the fragrant night breeze.

He tossed his keys on the table and turned to face her.

Kate's throat went dry. She met his eyes and years of shared history seemed to wrap itself around them, drawing them closer together until she was in his arms and the room, the hotel, even Paris fell away and all that was left was the two of them.

He tasted of coffee and cognac. Rich, deep, thrilling. She couldn't get enough of the feel of his mouth against hers. She was sixteen again and on fire for the only man she had ever loved.

CHAPTER SEVEN

THEY LEFT a trail of clothing from the foyer through the sitting room to the bedroom. By the time they fell together onto the bed, he was naked and she wore only ivory lace panties and red heels. She had never felt more powerful or sensual in her life.

His body was as familiar to her as her own. The muscular shoulders, the scar on his back from a diving accident, the smell of his skin. She would know him in the dark.

This was Paris. Paris wiped the slate clean if only for the night. While they were in that room, entwined together on that bed, they could be whoever they wanted to be.

No barriers. No boundaries. No limits. The warmth of cognac against her nipple...the moist heat of his tongue as he licked his way down her body...the raw male power that made her scream her pleasure in a way she never had before.

Anything was possible when there was no tomorrow.

They didn't talk. Words were dangerous. Words

could turn on you when you least expected it. They let their bodies say all those things they had kept hidden from each other for far too long.

The chemistry between them was undeniable. It had been from the beginning. But tonight, on that wide soft bed in Paris, their chemistry was touched by magic and the combination brought her to tears.

She turned her head away so he wouldn't see but he knew instantly.

"You're crying," he said, holding her close. "I didn't—"

She snuggled even closer. "You were wonderful. This was—" She searched for words to describe the way she was feeling, but they didn't exist in English or French or any other language.

"I know." He brushed his lips against her forehead. "For me too."

They had been careful this time. There would be no surprises nine months later to ruin a perfectly happy divorce.

Not that they talked about the divorce. By some unspoken agreement the divorce was off-limits tonight. They would do whatever it took to keep the fragile magic bubble of happiness aloft as long as they could.

They made love. They ate room-service croissants and washed them down with brandy and coffee. They made love again and then congratulated each other for proving you didn't have to be twenty-two to sizzle.

"Show me the portrait," he said as he handed her the last croissant.

"You'll see it at the wedding."

"How about a sneak peek."

"Maybe later."

"Come on," he said. "I'd really like to see it."

He almost backed off when he saw the uncertain look in her eyes, but then she swung her legs off the bed and motioned for him to follow her into the foyer.

He watched as she carefully unwrapped the painting from innumerable protective layers of paper and protective backing.

"The TSA got a preview at the airport," she said as she peeled away the last layer. "Raul and Melinda liked it but Sean and Paulie said it lacked nuance."

He laughed out loud and she smiled.

"I hope Alexis likes it. I didn't want to do one of those stiff and formal portraits. I tried to capture who we are—well, who we were." She turned it around to face him and the room fell silent.

She had painted their daughters on the back porch. Somehow she had caught them at an imaginary point between the girls they used to be and the women they were becoming. They were achingly lovely, his daughters, and ready to fly off into lives of their own. The way they leaned forward. The look in their eyes. Young women on the verge of their futures.

She had painted him into the upper right hand corner of the composition, watching over his daughters but no longer a part of their daily lives. She had chosen to paint herself as a reflection in the French doors behind the girls, a distracted but watchful presence with her easel and paints.

There was a bittersweet edge to the painting that he hadn't noticed before in her work. She had captured a family about to spin off into separate orbits. Alexis and Gabe would build a family of their own and one day soon Taylor and Shannon would follow suit. In a perfect world that would have marked the start of the second chapter in their married life, a renewal of all the early promises.

Instead they were standing on the brink of divorce.

How the hell could he have lived with her for so long, shared a bed and a life, and not come close to recognizing the depth of her talent? He had known she was good, but nothing had prepared him for this.

He felt he had been walking around blindfolded. He knew about the courses she had taken, the workshops, the day care she had bartered for art lessons, the careful management of their family budget so she could buy supplies. He knew it all. He had been there every step of the way. So why hadn't he been able to make the leap with her from passing interest to consuming passion? Why hadn't he seen her as the gifted artist she was and not just his wife?

"Say something, Ryan."

He was completely captured by the painting and the future unfolding for her. "Once that magazine article comes out, you're going to be on your way."

"You might be partial to the subject matter."

"This is the best thing you've ever done."

"Look at our girls. You couldn't possibly paint a bad portrait of them."

"Don't do that, Kate. This is great work. Admit it."

She hesitated then a huge smile spread across her face. "You're right," she said, tilting her head to one side as she inspected her work. "This *is* pretty damn good."

"That magazine article might change your life."

"We'll see. You never really know which way these things are going to go."

A thousand different emotions played across her familiar and beautiful face. He saw their history in her eyes. What he didn't see was their future.

"I was wrong."

She continued to look at him but said nothing.

"I expected you to jump when I got the job offer in Boston."

"So did I," she admitted. "I always said painting was portable. I just didn't know that I wasn't."

"We still could have made it work," he said. "I never gave us the chance."

She turned her head away and he couldn't tell if she was angry, sad, or had simply stopped hearing him a long time ago.

"You know what?" she said finally. "I probably wouldn't have listened. My contacts were all in New York. Everyone I knew, everyone I cared about. You might as well have asked me to move to Mars."

"I didn't ask," he said. "I announced."

She shot him a look. "Yeah, you kinda did just announce it."

But they both knew the problem went far deeper than that. They had drifted apart long before the Boston job offer. Work, kids, everyday life. Sometimes he thought they had scheduled themselves right out of their marriage.

But never out of love. For the first time in years, he finally understood that the love not only remained, it had flourished.

Now all he had to do was find a way to make her see that too.

TOWARD DAYBREAK it started to rain.

They had barely drifted off to sleep when it began, a steady tap-tap against the windows and eaves.

"I'll bet Aunt Celeste planned this, too," Kate said as Ryan got up to open the windows. The sweet smell of April rain and flowers filled the room.

If there was anything more romantic than being in bed with the man you loved on a rainy spring morning in Paris, she couldn't think what it might be.

"The deck's definitely stacked in favor of romance." He was standing by the window, looking down at the street traffic.

"Come back to bed," she murmured. "We just went to sleep a few minutes ago."

He bent down and placed a kiss against her temple and she sighed happily. "Don't worry," he whispered as she drifted back into sleep. "I'll be back in time for the wedding."

They didn't need the Louvre or the Eiffel Tower or the Champs d'Elysee.

Right now they had each other and that was everything.

KATE WOKE UP a little before eleven to an empty bed. It took a few seconds for her to remember that she wasn't home in her New York bed; she was in Paris.

With Ryan.

She touched his pillow with the back of her hand. It was cool. That was odd. She hadn't heard him get up.

The shirt he had worn yesterday was tossed over the side chair. She reached for it and slipped it on. It still smelled of him and she shivered with something close to pure animal pleasure.

The bathroom door was open, but there was no

sign of him there or in the sitting room. A funny little tingle of apprehension began to snake itself around her spine, but she pushed it away. He was a man and men could only go two or three hours without food. Maybe he had gone out in search of an Egg McMuffin or, better still, freshly baked croissants from one of those incredible bakeries that had been around since the Revolution.

She was about to go take a long hot shower when she decided to make sure the wedding portrait was safely tucked away, and she padded out to the foyer. The portrait had been neatly re-wrapped and returned to the huge travel portfolio. His cell phone was on the floor near the escritoire but his bags were nowhere to be seen.

Okay, she told herself as that uneasy tingle took hold again, this time with a vengeance. Every millennium or so, a man actually put his stuff away. Maybe this was one of those miracle moments. His cell probably fell out of his pocket when he bent down to stow his bags. She decided to play Nancy Drew for real this time and checked the foyer closet. It was empty. She ran back into the bedroom and checked the big double closet and it was empty too. There was nothing under the bed, hidden away behind the drapes or in the tub.

He was gone.

EPILOGUE

The Wedding
Milles Fleurs—the day before the wedding

"IT ISN'T AS IF he ran away, *chérie,*" Aunt Celeste said as she pulled another Gauloise Blonde from her vintage Chanel purse. "He did leave you a note."

Kate waved the square of hotel stationery under her great-aunt's nose. "'SomethingcameupI'llsee-youatMillesFleursinafewdaysdon'tworry' isn't a note. It's a telegram."

Her aunt flicked the wheel on her lighter then held the steady blue flame to the tip of her cigarette and inhaled three times in quick succession. "Wonderful flavor," she said, exhaling. "Are you sure you wouldn't care to try one?"

"I quit smoking ten years ago. It's a filthy habit. And don't change the subject. If you know where he is and you're not telling me—"

Celeste threw back her head and emitted one of those throaty laughs that had brought men to their knees back in the day. "You give me far too much credit, *chérie*. Ryan is his own man and he is about his own business. Be patient. He won't miss his daughter's wedding. He gave Alexis his word."

Whatever he was up to, he had taken time to make sure Alexis wouldn't worry. He had apparently dropped his bags off at Milles Fleurs and shared a long father-daughter breakfast with the bride-to-be. If Alexis was concerned about her father's whereabouts, she certainly didn't show it. She was happily navigating her way through the prewedding festivities without an apparent care in the world.

Selfishly, it was more than the wedding that concerned Kate. They had shared something special that night in the hotel suite. They had opened their hearts to each other for the first time in many years. For a little while she had actually believed there was hope for them, that he still loved her and that maybe they could start all over again.

The last thing she had expected was that he would run for his life.

"He'll come back," Kate said. "Won't he?"

Celeste patted her hand. "Don't be ridiculous. Of course he will."

"He said he'd be back in time for the wedding… at least I thought he did." At this point that entire magical day and night in Paris seemed like a dream. She turned to her aunt. "Something happened, Aunt Celeste. We opened up to each other. We said things we'd never said before. I felt closer to Ryan than I have since we were teen-agers, and I refuse to believe he didn't feel it, too."

"Then be patient," her aunt counseled. "Trust your heart."

Wasn't that how she got into this predicament in the first place?

"What if something happened to him?" she persisted. "I mean, he took his bags but left his cell phone behind. He's completely out of contact."

"I don't have one of those horrid things, either, *chérie,* and I always find a way to stay in touch. He's a grown man and quite resourceful. Enjoy the day before your daughter's wedding. He'll be back before you know it." She took Kate's hand in hers and squeezed. "I promise you this."

Who was Kate to argue? When it came to love, Aunt Celeste wrote the book. If Celeste said to trust her heart, then she would give it her best shot.

But if there was no word from Ryan by dinner tonight, then, with apologies to her great-aunt, she would feel free to panic.

One hour before the wedding

"HE'S ON HIS WAY, Mom." Alexis, the picture of radiant loveliness in her bridal gown, handed Kate a tissue. "He borrowed the cab driver's cell phone and called the inn."

Kate, who really hadn't intended or expected to

fall apart quite like this, blew her nose. "Where has he been? Why didn't he call sooner? What happened? Is he okay?"

"He's fine." Her little girl—wasn't it yesterday she wore her hair in a ponytail and watched reruns of *Little House on the Prairie?*—gave her a hug. "It's okay, Mom. Admit it—you can't wait to see him again."

She looked at her daughter, glowing with love and joy, and knew she couldn't lie to her. Not today. "You're right, honey. I can't wait."

Her emotions were in complete shambles. She swung from crazed worry to elation to almost murderous rage then back again. He had no business taking off like that on a moment's notice. He had no business not phoning for days and worrying her to death. But he was alive and well and on his way to Milles Fleurs and at the moment that simple fact outweighed everything else.

The bridesmaids burst into the side parlor room in an explosion of pale peach and spring-green silk and taffeta, bringing the scent of flowers and happiness with them. She had watched these girls all of their lives, celebrated their birthdays and graduations and first jobs. Those adorable little girls had grown up to be beautiful, accomplished young women who were gathered here today on the outskirts of the City of Light to celebrate Alexis and Gabe's wedding. The fact that two of those beautiful young women were also her daughters pushed her right over the edge into another bout of sentimental tears.

"This has to stop, Ma." This time Taylor handed her some tissues.

"Even waterproof mascara has its limits," Shannon said as she adjusted the flowers pinned to her hair. "Better save some of its staying power for the ceremony."

"The heck with the ceremony," Alexis said. "Just wait for the first dance. When she and Daddy take the floor—"

"Did I hear my name?"

Kate spun around to see Ryan standing in the doorway to the side parlor room. His daughters threw themselves into his arms. The other girls cheered. There seemed to be no broken bones, no gunshot wounds, no visible sign of injury or illness. Relief almost brought her to her knees, but plain old anger lifted her right back up again.

At least now she could kill him with a clear conscience.

The wedding coordinator, imported from New York, appeared in the doorway and motioned the bride and her attendants into the adjoining room for a final inspection before the ceremony, which was to take place in the garden underneath a large white tent turned makeshift chapel.

"Get yourselves ready, bride's parents," she said with a big smile. "It's almost showtime."

"Showtime?" Ryan said after the woman disappeared into the other room.

He looked exhausted, unsure of himself, clearly waiting for the laugh she couldn't give to him.

"Okay," he said. "Here it is." He met her eyes. "I was arrested."

She could feel the blood drain from her head. "You were what?"

"Arrested. I flew back to New York. I thought I could get there and back in twenty-four, but I got arrested breaking into our old house."

"I have to sit down," she said, perching on the straight-back chair in the corner of the tiny room. "For a second I thought you said you'd been arrested."

"I broke into the house and forgot about the silent alarm. The entire Levittown police force showed up when I was elbow-deep in your desk drawer."

She didn't know whether to laugh, cry, or ask for a good stiff drink.

"Remember Bernie Cowan?"

"The lawyer on your softball team."

"I tracked him down on a fishing boat off Montauk Point. He's the only reason I'm not still in the Nassau County jail."

"You have a set of keys. Why didn't you use them?"

"I left them in my bag."

"One of the bags you dropped off here at the inn?"

"Bingo."

"And you couldn't call because you left your cell phone in the hotel room."

"So that's where it is." The cell phone also functioned as his address book, phone book and appointment calendar. He was screwed without it.

"Your cell isn't the only phone on the planet."

"I'm forty-eight," he said with a self-deprecating laugh. "I couldn't remember the name of the damn place." He moved closer to her, so close she could smell his skin. "You have a lot of questions, Katie, but you haven't asked me the most important one."

It took a long moment before she found her voice. "Why?" One word with their entire future wrapped up in it.

She held her breath as he reached into the breast pocket of his tux.

"I went back for this."

He held out his hand and there in the palm was a small circle of gold.

She met his eyes. "My wedding ring?"

"It was in your sock drawer. Took me three hours to find it."

"How did you even know it was in the house?"

He told her about the letter from Alexis right after the engagement party.

"And you remembered."

He nodded. "I remembered."

"I love you," she said, choking back her tears. "I never stopped."

"I've loved you from the first day we met, Katie. Without you life doesn't make sense."

She looked at the ring on his left hand and smiled. "You never took yours off?" she asked. "Not even once?"

"Why would I? I'm a married man."

She held out her own left hand and he slid the ring back onto her finger. "And I'm a married woman."

"For better or for worse," he said.

"Until death do us part," she whispered.

He drew her into his arms and they were about to seal the promise with a kiss when they realized their three daughters were watching them from the doorway.

"Well, it's about time," Shannon said.

"Took you long enough," Taylor chimed in. "We were wondering when you two would realize how much you loved each other."

"This is the best wedding present in the world." Alexis was radiant with joy. "I knew Paris would work its magic on you."

They didn't have the heart to tell her that Paris had had a little help from Aunt Celeste.

"It's time, everyone! Let's hurry!" the wedding coordinator called out. "The flower girls are already moving."

This was the reason for everything, Kate thought. This was why men and women fell in love, why they married, why they endured the tough times and the disappointments. You did it for your children, so they could grow up knowing the wonderful safety net called family and have the courage to walk out into the world with an open heart, fall in love and start the whole wonderful cycle all over again.

And if you were very lucky, when the kids were gone and the house was quiet once again, your best friend and lover was still there, waiting to discover what wonderful surprises the future held in store for the two of you. It could be Boston. It could be New York. It could even be Paris. Maybe they would buy a boat and sail away together to some tropical paradise where she would paint and he would write. Anything was possible. The future was theirs for the taking and Kate couldn't wait to see where it would lead them.

Shannon and Taylor joined the other bridesmaids for the long walk down the aisle. Alexis took her place between her parents and squeezed their hands.

"I can't believe this is really happening," she said.

"Well, it is," Kate said. "It's your wedding day."

"Not that," Alexis said. "I mean, I can't believe you and Daddy are finally back together."

Kate and Ryan looked at each other and thirty

years of shared history passed between them in an instant and with it the promise of at least thirty more.

"We're back together," Ryan said.

"Forever," Kate said.

"But there's one more thing," Alexis said.

"Honey, the music started out there. We have to—"

Alexis was her mother's daughter and she stopped Kate mid-sentence. "I'm the bride. They can't start without me. You two renewed your vows before, but you didn't seal it with a kiss."

They were in each other's arms in an instant.

The kiss was sweet and it held within it everything they were and all they would become. The two years apart seemed to vanish as if they had never happened and for the first time Kate felt happy again. She was back where she belonged.

The strains of the "Wedding March" flooded the small room and they moved away from each other to flank their daughter. Through the open door they saw a handsome and very nervous Gabe Fellini waiting at the altar for his first glimpse of his bride.

And that was how a family began. A nervous groom, a radiant bride, sweet promises that took years to fully understand and a lifetime to keep. Friends come and friends go. Your children grow up and move away. Careers soar and then fall apart. But through it all, the one you loved was right there by your side, sharing the sorrows and multiplying the joys.

If Alexis and Gabe had that, they would have everything.

Just like Kate and Ryan.

SOMETHING BORROWED, SOMETHING BLUE

Marie Ferrarella

To
Marsha Zinberg
With Many Thanks

CHAPTER ONE

Six days before the wedding

PARIS, THE CITY OF LIGHT. Paris, the City For Lovers.

Bah, humbug.

The disgruntled thought echoed through Shannon Donovan's brain as the plane she'd boarded at New York's JFK Airport several hours ago began to lower its landing gear. Her international flight was approaching its destination.

Finally.

It seemed as if she'd been in the air forever. Or maybe it was just that her feelings had been up in the air during the entire flight. Up in the air and as upset as she'd ever been in all of her twenty-nine years.

Dark thoughts were not the norm for Shannon and this was supposed to be a happy occasion. Her younger sister, Alexis, was getting married in Paris in six days. And, up until a little over twenty-four hours ago, Shannon *had* been happy. Happy for Alexis, happy for herself and happy that both her parents, separated for these past few years, had both actually agreed to attend the festivities.

Twenty-four hours ago, she'd thought, no, she was positive, that the seat next to her would be occupied by Robert Newhall. *Her* Robert.

The man who had given her the small but brilliant heart-shaped diamond ring on the third finger of her left hand.

However, at the very last possible minute, Robert had stunned her. Just as she was set to go to the airport, Robert had called on her cell phone to tell her that he wasn't coming to Paris. His excuse was that he was right in the middle of a court case he couldn't abandon. She had gotten a leave of absence from her law firm, but he couldn't do the same with his.

She wasn't all that sure she believed him, which *really* bothered her. Lately, there had been signs, signs she didn't want to acknowledge, that maybe the man she was all set to spend the rest of her life with wasn't as trustworthy as she'd thought.

Paris was supposed to fix that. To cast out the doubts and rekindle the romance.

Instead, here she was, six days away from what was to be the biggest day of Alexis's life, feeling lost and alone. Lost and alone despite the fact that over half the plane seemed to be filled with people bound for the Donovan-Fellini wedding. Although her parents were both flying out later, onboard the plane was her youngest sister, Taylor, who was attempting to hide the fact that she was completely starry-eyed about this trip to the romance capital of the world, and, of course, Alexis, the woman they were all doing this for.

There were a number of Alexis's friends on the flight as well. The rest of the voluminous crowd was comprised of what she'd come to regard as groom Gabriel Fellini's posse.

Shannon could swear that the noise Gabe's family generated had been almost nonstop since the moment they'd been declared airborne. You'd think that this flight from New York to Paris was a private jet, what with Fellini siblings, cousins, uncles, aunts and assorted friends continually insisting on visiting with one another and cluttering up the aisles as they meandered back and forth. This had to be the only flight she'd ever been on where the turbulence inside the plane far exceeded anything found outside the plane.

As the plane continued descending, Alexis, who, along with Gabe, was seated in front of Shannon, twisted around to look at her. "Smile," her sister ordered with a laugh. "We're almost there, Shannon." Alexis suddenly frowned. "I never knew you hated to fly so much," she finally declared.

Because Shannon didn't want to discuss why Robert wasn't there, a fact that had, because of the crowd, still escaped Alexis's notice, Shannon forced a smile to her lips.

Ever since her sister had been six, Alexis had dreamed of a big, fancy wedding with all the trimmings—years before Alexis had even decided that she liked boys. The first few years, when she, Alexis and Taylor had played "pretend," she'd had to take the part of the groom because she was taller. Taylor played multiple roles, being the ring bearer or the flower girl or, as she grew taller, one of the bridesmaids.

The idea of a big, fancy *Paris* wedding didn't evolve until around the time Alexis turned thirteen. It was referred to around the Donovan household as Alexis's French period. Alexis became obsessed with all things French or springing from French origins. Alexis even went as far as studying the language in high school when everyone around her was learning Spanish.

It seemed to Shannon that Alexis had been awaiting this big event all of her life. So when Alexis had asked her to be maid of honor, she was thrilled. As the oldest, and blessed—or cursed— with a type-A personality, she took her duties seriously.

But not having Robert here was going to be a definite damper.

You'd think that a man who was working so hard and doing so well at the law firm where he was employed could take a little time off to fly to Paris with his fiancée for a major family event.

But when she made the point to him during that fateful cell-phone call, Robert had certainly put her in her place. "Damn it, Shannon, don't be such a drama queen. You know I'm up for partner this time around and this case could just be my ticket in. I thought you were proud of me."

"I am." *It's just that I want you to be here in Paris with me, to see my sister married. To propose to me somewhere more romantic than the lobby of our building, in front of an elevator with an Out Of Order sign.*

"I'll make it up to you," he told her in a tone that said he wasn't to be questioned or pushed. "I promise. We'll go to Paris some other time."

For one wild, unthinking moment, she'd even offered to remain behind to act as Robert's cheering section and provide him with moral support.

"What, and have your family hate me for the rest of my life because you weren't there to see Alexis get married? Not a chance. Go. Enjoy yourself. And think of me once in a while, slaving away in a hot courtroom, making a name for myself. For us."

The last part had almost seemed forced, but she told herself she was imagining things. So, she'd banked down her disappointment, wished him well and gone to the airport alone, barely making the flight in time.

But disappointment crept up on her now, as the plane was landing.

She had to snap out of it, Shannon upbraided herself. Her sister needed her. Besides, this was Paris. Paris, the city of magic.

The smile Shannon offered her sister as the plane's wheels touched the Paris runway was far more genuine than the one she'd summoned a scarce few seconds ago.

"That's better," Alexis declared, turning back around and sliding down into her seat.

Alexis, Shannon thought fondly, had apparently begun celebrating her upcoming nuptials a wee bit ahead of schedule.

"I KNOW THAT WOMAN, Gabe."

Surprise underlined each syllable Josh McClintock uttered as he glanced through the open door of the Milles Fleurs Inn at the crowd converging around the small front desk. Despite the numerous people clustered about a very harried desk clerk, Josh had zeroed in on the extremely attractive woman standing to the right of his best friend's bride. Zeroed in on her and had something remote click in his brain that sent waves akin to déjà vu through his entire system.

Surrounded by his parents, three brothers, four

sisters and their assorted families, all of whom seemed intent on getting through the doorway at the exact same moment, Gabe Fellini barely suppressed an impatient sigh. Abandoning his plea for his family to move one at a time through the door's opening, Gabe began physically shepherding his immediate family into the quaint inn. Rooms at the inn had been reserved for them by his fiancée's great-aunt Celeste Beaulieu, who lived in the area. It was obvious to him that Great-Aunt Celeste apparently had no concept of physics and the law about just what could occupy a single space at any given time.

As he gently ushered his mother, Audrey, through the doorway, Gabe spared Josh, his best friend as well as his best man, a testy look. Fighting last-minute wedding jitters while simultaneously dealing with his boisterous family did not put him in the right frame of mind to put up with Josh's notorious roving eye.

"You know every woman, Josh." Flashing an automatic smile at his sister Gina, Gabe placed his hand to the small of her back and moved her into the inn after his mother. "Isn't it time you found a new line?"

But for once, there was no wicked gleam in Josh's eye as he continued looking into the inn and at the woman who had caught not only his attention but stirred his memory. Memories that went all the way back to high school. He aligned himself with Gabe, moving out of the way of the continuous stream of people heading in.

"No," he insisted, "I'm serious. I *know* her. The tall one with the great legs and red hair."

Looking toward where Josh was pointing, Gabe immediately saw who Josh was referring to. "Oh, no."

"Oh, no, what?"

Gabe stepped aside as more of his family filed past him and into the inn's foyer. As he did so, he grabbed Josh by the arm, pulling the handsome blond-haired man with him. Urgently. "Oh, no, you don't know her." He clenched his teeth, straining out the rest of the words and wrapping them in a warning. "I won't let you know her. Understand?"

Josh looked at his taller, ordinarily easygoing friend. "Why?"

"Because," Gabe lowered his voice, "that's Alexis's sister, Shannon. Members of Alexis's family are off-limits to you, Josh. That includes both of her sisters and her mother. Do I make myself clear?"

Ever the lighthearted charmer, Josh dramatically placed a hand over his chest. "You wound me, Gabe. Deeply."

There wasn't a hint of a smile on Gabe's dark, handsome face as he promised, "I'll wound you seriously if you make a play for Shannon—or Taylor," he added for good measure. Taylor was the baby of the family, only twenty-two years old, but there was no reason to think that kept her safe from Josh's charms. "Paris is full of women, find yourself one. Besides, Shannon is engaged."

The news only brought a moment's thoughtful pause to his friend as the latter nodded at the last of Gabe's siblings crossing the inn's threshold. "She's not married yet, is she?"

Gabe looked as if he was debating answering before he finally, reluctantly, released the fatal word. "No."

Josh flashed a smile that could have lit up the entire borough of Queens, New York where they both originated from. "Then she's fair game." He looked at Gabe. "Did you say 'Shannon'?"

There was a leery expression on Gabe's face as he entered the building behind Josh. "Yes."

"Shannon Donovan. Of course."

Gabe wove his way to the front of the crowd near the front desk. "If you just had an epiphany, spare me the details until I get everyone registered here," he told Josh just before the questions from his siblings and cousins became almost deafening.

Josh stepped back. Gabe looked like a man drowning, he thought, compassion stirring within him. Compassion, but not empathy. A harried groom-to-be was something he was never going to be. Or at least, not for another decade or so. Marriage was not something he even remotely contemplated at this point in his life. Not that Gabe's fiancée, Alexis, wasn't a terrific girl and all that, but he firmly believed that men shouldn't marry until they were in their forties.

It took at least that long to narrow down the field, he mused, looking over his shoulder through the still open doorway as a few of the local young women drifted by, chattering and laughing.

Life was definitely too short, he thought not for the first time.

As first Gabe, whose French was limited to a handful of words, and then Alexis tried to make the nervous-looking clerk understand that they all needed accommodations and had assumed they'd booked individual rooms for everyone, Josh looked back over to the tall, slender redhead. She looked removed from what was going on around her, as if she were there in body but not in spirit. As he drew closer to her he wondered why there was such a sad look in her eyes.

For all his reputation, Josh was not a woman-izer. He thought of himself as a woman-enjoyer. He never took advantage of a woman, never used lies to talk his way into a woman's bed. Everything was clear and aboveboard in his relationships right from the start. He possessed a healthy conscience.

And a healthy memory. He knew—although he

would never admit it, not even to Gabe—what it felt like to fall in love and hold nothing but empty dreams in your hand.

He edged a little closer still, nodding at one of Gabe's cousins in passing, never taking his eyes off the target. It was her all right.

Shannon Donovan.

The one who got away.

Not that, as far as he knew, she was actually even slightly aware of that fact. Back in high school, he'd been a completely different person. He'd been short, still waiting for the growth spurt his father kept promising would come but didn't happen until he'd turned nineteen. He'd been painfully withdrawn back then. Not like Shannon. Shannon Donovan had been his total opposite. Outgoing, vibrant. Cheerleader, class president, captain of the debating team. And gorgeous. Drop-dead, oh-my-heart-hurts gorgeous. From the top of her red hair to the bottom of her perfectly shaped toes, she stopped traffic and men's hearts.

She'd been, in his estimation, the perfect woman. And so out of his league he might as well have resided on another planet. His only contact with her had been math class. If he hadn't loved math already, he would have then. He lived for sixth period precalculus. The subject seemed to be the only one Shannon ever had trouble with, while for him, it was easy, like breathing. He'd tutored her in the library for three glorious months that ended all too soon. After that, her math requirement was over and so was their association, except for the brief minutes when she'd stopped to sign his senior yearbook and asked him to sign hers. He'd been so stunned he couldn't think of anything more to say than "Remember precalculus?"

He'd spent the next few days calling himself an idiot and the next several years changing himself into someone else. After his growth spurt finally arrived, he joined a gym, took dance lessons on the sly and eventually came into his own as his career on Wall Street took off.

Success had made a new man of him, giving him confidence and helping him see himself in a more positive light. He decided to make up for lost time and throw himself into the social whirl. He and Gabe, whom he met on his first day at Pride and Wasserman, the brokerage firm they both worked for, had been inseparable for a while. Then Gabe had met Alexis and stopped playing the field.

But not Josh. He'd finally come into his own. He was not about to give that freedom up for anyone.

However, seeing Shannon took him back to the past. It was as if someone had opened a time portal, suddenly whisking him to his senior year in high school, a time when he'd been awkward, tongue-tied and ill at ease.

Josh took a deep breath. Squaring his shoulders, he moved farther away from Gabe, who was far too entrenched in relatives and language difficulties, to disengage himself long enough to grab Josh's arm and pull him back this time.

Moving next to Shannon, Josh paused to take another breath. Her perfume was something light, yet seductive. It suited her.

He poured every ounce of his acquired charm into his greeting as he put out his hand. "Hi, I'm Josh McClintock, friend of the groom."

Turning, Shannon smiled then put out her own hand. "Shannon Donovan, sister of the bride." And then, as her hand made contact with his, her eyes widened and there was a flicker of recognition. "What did you say your name was?"

"Josh McClintock."

"Joshua?" she asked incredulously. Her green eyes narrowed a little bit as she concentrated. "Did you attend William Cullen Bryant High School?"

Why the hell did his heart just do that funny little thing that, had he been three decades older, would have had him searching for the phone number of the nearest reputable cardiologist? He did his best to look nonchalant. "In Queens? Yes, I did."

Shannon's smile widened. His erratic cardiac activity continued. "You probably don't remember me, but you saved my butt."

His breath backed up in his lungs as he contemplated that part of her anatomy. "Excuse me?"

He was rewarded with a laugh that sent hot ripples over his skin. He realized he was still holding her hand and released it.

"You tutored me in precalculus. If it wasn't for you, I would have failed," she said.

"Then you wouldn't have been valedictorian."

Pleasure highlighted her delicate heart-shaped face. "Then you do remember me."

"How could I forget someone like you?"

God, but she wished Robert felt that way.

Josh saw the sadness return. "I'm sorry, did I say something wrong?"

"No, you said something right," she told him. "Something very right."

For a moment, he was Joshua again, tongue-tied and as awkward as a puppy that hadn't grown into its feet. He purposely glanced down at her hand and said the first thing that came to his head. "So, are you next?"

Delicate eyebrows gathered together in confusion over green eyes that had haunted his dreams for a year after graduation. "Next?"

He nodded, then indicated her left hand. "To get married."

She raised her engagement ring up as if she hadn't seen it before. "Oh. Yes."

There was something odd about the way she gave her answer—automatically and quickly, as if to cover a nervousness. Something was not completely right in paradise, he thought. Josh glanced around for a man making a beeline for them. No one was. "So, where's your fiancé?"

Shannon sighed. "Back in New York."

"Later flight?" His expression was purposely innocent. Inside, his heart had accelerated again.

Shannon shook her head. "He's not coming."

"Really?" Josh did his best to suppress a grin. In his estimation, destiny had just suddenly opened up a very big door and laid down a welcome mat before him.

CHAPTER TWO

SHANNON DIDN'T REMEMBER Joshua being this tall or this good-looking when they were back in high school together. She did, however, remember his eyes. He'd always had beautiful blue eyes. Sincere eyes, she'd thought at the time. Now, they seemed like eyes that would make a woman forget herself.

What was the matter with her? What kind of thoughts was she having here? She was engaged, for heaven's sake. Just because Robert wasn't here didn't change anything.

And where is he? Is he really working or…?

She blamed her doubts and confusion on stress and fatigue and the irritating din that refused to abate. If anything, the volume was getting louder. There were now several more people around the front desk and they were all talking at once.

This did not look good, Shannon thought. Time to stop thinking about herself and ride to the rescue, if that was possible.

She flashed a smile in Josh's direction, effectively terminating any further conversation. "Excuse me, I think my sister needs me."

Easing herself away from Josh and the momentary detour she'd taken down memory lane, Shannon made her way over to Alexis and the other wedding guests. She had always been the problem solver in her family, the one who'd looked at all the scattered, broken pieces and found a way to pick them up again in order to make them fit long after everyone else had given up. It was one of the reasons she made such a good lawyer.

"Need help?" Josh asked, showing absolutely no indication that he was about to fade into the flowered wallpaper even if she turned him down.

Yes, please.

But though the automatic response echoed in her head, Shannon didn't take the time to answer him. Every second counted. She knew what Alexis was like when she came apart at the seams. It didn't happen often, but it was not a pretty sight.

Burrowing her way to the front of the mob scene, Shannon placed one comforting arm around Alexis and smiled winningly at the man behind the front desk.

"What's wrong, honey?" she asked her sister.

Alexis stared at her dumbfounded, as if she couldn't see how anyone could not know what was happening here—the disintegration of civilization as it was known in its present state.

"What's wrong?" Alexis echoed incredulously. "What's wrong?"

"That's what I asked." Shannon did her best to sound cheerful and patient. In her experience, drama had never been the way to solve any problem.

There were tears beginning to form in Alexis's eyes. Her sister gestured toward the man behind the desk as if his sole purpose in life was to ruin her dream wedding.

"What's wrong is that no one told me that this inn was long on charm and short on rooms."

"We have rooms, *mademoiselle,*" the clerk retorted with no small indignation. "We just do not have as many as you would like."

Shannon focused her attention on the clerk. "How many do you have? Unoccupied," she added, in case the man thought she was just taking random inventory.

The answer came with no hesitation, no pause to mentally take a count. "Twenty-five. I have twenty-five rooms. I have emp-teed the en-tire inn for your wed-ding," he announced, drawing out the words to add emphasis to the trial he had endured. There was petulance in every elongated syllable.

"Twenty-five," Alexis cried in disbelief. "We've got at least seventy people."

Probably more, Shannon thought. Alexis had

never been good with numbers. But for the sake of peace, she focused on the only solution immediately available. "So? We'll just triple up."

Gabe frowned. Easygoing to a fault, it was clear that he had severe reservations about this suggestion. His eyes swept over a number of his cousins. Shannon could almost see what he was thinking—Mayday!

"Triple up? Shannon, that really might not be the best way to go."

"Right now, that's the *only* way to go. Besides," she said, doing her best to sound upbeat and positive, "this is *Paris*. We didn't come here to stay cooped up in a room. We came to celebrate your happiness and to take in the sights." She gestured toward the group. "Most of these people will be out all night. If anything, we'll need the rooms to change clothes in, to take a quick catnap before we're up and out again." She turned toward Alexis. "This is what you wanted, right, Alexis? To be in Paris, to get a feel for the city and soak it up. You can kick back in a hotel room in any city in the world. This is Paris, made to be enjoyed up close and personal—*outside* of an inn," she emphasized.

In response, she saw relief on her future brother-in-law's ruggedly handsome face. A smile was beginning to form on her sister's lips.

Success, Shannon thought.

Having temporarily quelled Alexis and Gabe's

misgivings, Shannon turned toward the others. She clapped her hands together for attention, first once, then again. Nothing happened. And then, behind her, a piercing whistle tore the air. When she turned, Josh winked at her.

"Just trying to help," he told her.

It did the trick. The wedding guests settled down long enough for her to talk. "People, I want you to choose two other people you won't mind hearing snore. Due to a slight misunderstanding about the number of rooms available, we'll be sleeping three to a room. The rooms will just be for resting anyway, so please make your roommate choices and let's get registered. Paris is waiting."

To her relief, Shannon saw people gathering into groups. It looked as if her suggestion was taking hold. She saw a few distant relatives she knew for a fact hadn't been on speaking terms discuss sharing a room.

Stunned, Shannon turned toward Alexis, who was beaming at her with relief. Shannon inclined her head toward her sister. "I thought this was Paris, not Lourdes."

"Lourdes?" Alexis echoed, confused.

"The place of miracles," Josh answered.

He was standing behind her again. Shannon turned around and her smile widened.

It looked, he thought, every bit as beatific as the one that had haunted his dreams that first full year after graduation. "We're on the same wavelength," Shannon said, amused.

"You have no idea." He knew that he'd never uttered truer words in his life.

He was a great deal more charming and confident than he used to be, Shannon caught herself thinking. The next moment, she turned her attention back to Alex and where she was needed.

"How DID I WIND UP with you?" Taylor asked petulantly. She kicked aside the purse she'd just tripped over while trying to get to a closet that could only generously be referred to as moderately adequate. Taylor punctuated her question with a huff and a deep sigh.

Shannon gave her a smile that was all teeth but little feeling. Not because she didn't love Taylor—she and the family did. But right now, she was in no mood for her baby sister's flashes of temper or her spoiled behavior, something, she knew, they were all guilty of having fostered a couple of decades ago when Taylor had been probably the most adorable baby under the sun.

"Just lucky, I guess," Shannon told Taylor. And, Shannon supposed, in her estimation, Taylor actually was lucky. There were only two of them to this room rather than three as in most of the other rooms. Which was a good thing, she thought. With both of them in the room, there was hardly enough space for air, much less another person.

The frown on Taylor's face as she made her return trip to the open suitcase on the double bed indicated that she didn't share that opinion. "Lucky would be if I was sharing the room with one of those cute Fellini cousins," Taylor replied.

"Which cousin?" Shannon asked.

Taylor shook her head. "Doesn't matter. All of them." Then she flashed the wicked smile that had kept her father up nights when Taylor was in high school.

Taylor still needed a keeper, Shannon thought wearily. "Try to be good, Taylor."

The wicked smile only grew that much wider. Raising her eyebrows, she twirled a long blond curl around her finger. "I always try to be good."

Nope, Shannon thought, she wasn't going to do it. She wasn't going to spend the next six days babysitting Taylor until the wedding took place. Taylor was twenty-two. She was old enough to look out for herself—and to suffer the consequences of her actions.

The resolution sounded good in theory, but Shannon still heard herself saying, "I meant good as in 'Goody Two-shoes,' not as in 'a good time was had by all.'"

To her surprise, her sister snorted. "You should talk."

Shannon stopped putting away her own things into the minuscule bureau. Her eyes narrowed as she looked at her sister. "And what's that supposed to mean?"

Taylor looked like the cat that had just dined on a canary feast. "I saw you getting chummy with the best man."

"We happen to be old friends, Taylor, nothing more," she said simply. "Joshua and I went to high school together."

The smirk on Taylor's lips testified that she was far from convinced. "Does Robert know about this 'old friend'?"

Shannon sighed, carefully hanging up her maid-of-honor dress in what she'd taken as her side of the tiny closet. "Robert doesn't know about anything but work." The instant the words left her lips, she regretted them. She was nothing if not loyal and that was an extremely disloyal remark, brought on by a tiny burst of resentment. "That wasn't fair."

Taylor shrugged carelessly, dismissing her guilt. Her sister had never liked Robert and was not the type to keep her opinion to herself. "If you ask me, this Josh guy's a lot cuter."

Because she'd fleetingly thought that herself, Shannon felt enormously guilty, never mind that she suspected Robert wasn't as faithful as he pretended to be. "Nobody asked."

Just as she said it, there was a knock on the door. Shannon worked her way through the obstacle course of Taylor's remaining suitcases, fighting the urge to ask why a six-day stay should require the need for three jam-packed suitcases.

The door stuck as she tried to open it. Shannon tugged hard and nearly fell backward as success greeted her on her second attempt.

Strong hands went out to steady her, and shock rippled through her, their point of origin being just beneath Josh's hands.

"Speak of the devil," Taylor murmured under her breath, clearly pleased as she peered around her sister's shoulder.

"Were you?" Josh asked, withdrawing his hands from Shannon's arms. "Speaking of the devil?" he added when Shannon stared at him in confusion.

Still dealing with the unnerving reaction she'd just had to his touch, Shannon did her best to pull herself together. She tossed what she hoped was a careless glance toward her sister.

"Don't pay any attention to Taylor—she's still in the rough-formation stage. Something wrong with your room?" she asked, coming to the only conclusion for his unexpected appearance at her door. For some reason, although this was Alexis and Gabe's wedding and Great-Aunt Celeste had been the one in charge of finding this place, everyone seemed to think that she was in charge of this event because she'd helped sort out the room-shortage problem.

Story of her life, Shannon thought with a degree of resignation.

She watched as a smile slowly unfolded along Josh's lips. Behind her, she could almost feel Taylor radiating approval and interest. She did her best to block Taylor's view.

"Now that you mention it," Josh replied, "yes, there is something wrong with my room."

Not that she could do anything about it, Shannon thought, but it only seemed polite to ask. "What?"

"The view."

His eyes swept over her and she had the distinct feeling of being touched. All over. She'd never felt quite this strangely vulnerable before. Jet lag? Paris? Feeling sorry for herself? Had to be one of those three, none of which had anything to do with the good-looking man whose presence coincided with the formation of multiple goose bumps on her flesh.

"It's much better here," Josh was saying, his eyes sweeping over her face. And then he grinned. "But that's not why I'm here."

Damn it, now she felt a blush forming. Just what she needed. Shannon cleared her throat and tried to sound distant. She succeeded only marginally. "I don't mean to sound rude, but why *are* you here?"

"To take you up on your sightseeing suggestion."

Shannon drew a blank. All that they had talked

about was high school and math. Was she forgetting something? "Excuse me?"

He was nothing if not genial. Robert, when pressed, would snap out his responses, as if she were stealing from him precious time that couldn't be replaced.

Why was she doing this? she upbraided herself. Why was she comparing Robert to other men when she was beyond that stage? As if to ground herself, she fingered the back of her engagement ring with her thumb.

"Earlier in the lobby," Josh told her, "when you were quelling the masses, you said we were here to take in the sights. I thought you might like some company." He raised his eyes toward Taylor. "Unless you've made other arrangements—"

She had a sharp, legal mind, able to remember and summon the most obscure details at will to back up arguments. She took pride in the fact that she could think on her feet. Why, then, did her brain feel like leftover mush that had been standing on a stove for three days?

Shannon looked at Taylor's suitcase on the floor, grasping for straws. "Well, um, I was just about to unpack—"

"Go," Taylor urged, placing both hands against her back and all but pushing her out the door. "I can unpack for you."

Okay, maybe there was no harm in going sightseeing with Joshua. After all, he *was* an old friend. Shannon looked down at what she was wearing. She'd put on a pair of jeans and an old hunter-green tank top because the room was so warm.

"I'd have to change," she began a little uncertainly.

"Why?"

She spread her hands before her. "You don't want to be seen with me like this."

He grinned. "Ask me."

Was it the heat in the room? Joshua seemed to be fairly radiating with sensuality. *Why didn't you come with me, Robert?* Again, she glanced down at her outfit. Somehow, it just didn't seem to fit with Paris. It fit with sitting in a hotel room, counting minutes until the ordeal she was faced with was over.

"It doesn't bother you that I look like I'm cleaning out the garage?"

"My garage should be so lucky." He took Shannon's hand and drew her across the threshold as if he were gently coaxing her along a tightrope wire. "Come on, Paris is waiting."

As Shannon turned, Taylor tossed her purse to her. "You heard the man, don't keep Paris waiting."

The next moment, the door was firmly shut behind her.

Talk about obvious, Shannon thought in dismay. She knew that Taylor disliked Robert, but this was really awkward. "She'd do anything for a little privacy."

Headed for the stairs, Josh laughed. "I know exactly how your sister feels. I'm in a room with two of the Fellini cousins that I'm not quite sure made it onto the evolutionary chart."

She bit her lower lip, trying not to laugh. "You know, there are other places to stay besides this inn."

They were drifting down the stairs now and he was completely focused on her as he shook his head. "Short notice."

Maybe, but there had to be a room somewhere. A decent-size one. She imagined that money wouldn't be a factor for someone as successful as Gabe had told her his best friend was. "They can't all be booked."

"This is the busy season as far as tourism goes and besides, the wedding is taking place here." Reaching the bottom of the stairs, he shrugged nonchalantly. "So it's a little inconvenient. It's only for six days. I've been in worse conditions."

The rooms were small, basically airless and, from what she'd sampled, the mattresses doubled as rock beds for the local flower gardens. "Been to prison, have you?" she quipped.

He laughed again. She found the sound warm and oddly thrilling. "You still have the same sense of humor," he noted.

Not lately, she thought. Thinking back about

the past few months, she realized that she'd had precious little to find funny. Life with Robert was so serious, so focused, so driven. It had taken the humor out of life.

But she wasn't about to complain about Robert or even mentally list his shortcomings. She knew that was only the hurt feelings talking. Robert was a good, decent man who was going places. He needed her.

She smiled at Josh and nodded. "Some things never change." She took a deep breath as they walked out the front door. "So, what would you like to see first?"

"I'll leave that up to you."

She had no idea why that sent another warm shiver up and down her spine. But it did.

CHAPTER THREE

WHEN SHANNON AND Josh decided to take in the Eiffel Tower, Paris's most famous symbol, after first seeing the Arc de Triomphe, Shannon had suggested they go the usual tourist route and take a tour along with the group of people gathering near a booth.

But Josh quickly vetoed the idea. "Where's your sense of adventure?" he challenged.

These days, she liked things laid out for her, all neatly fitted into their proper categories. Josh was, she knew, remembering the Shannon she used to be. The one who had tackled life full-tilt. The one who'd love to have fun.

When had that stopped?

Even as the question came to her, she refused to examine the all-too-painful reply.

Instead, she shifted her eyes to Josh's face. The look in his eyes was magnetic and too hard to resist. "Just what do you have in mind?"

Her question brought an answer to his mind that he knew was best kept to himself. Because what he was thinking had nothing to do with an age-old Parisian symbol and everything to do with her. "Exploring the tower on our own," he told her. "Without a guide." Putting an arm around her, he drew her away from a crowd that was getting ready to do just the opposite of what he was suggesting. "We can pretend we're natives, that the tower is practically in our backyard, a sight to be taken in every day and taken for granted." He winked as he took her hand in his, leading her to an elevator. "Like New Yorkers with the Empire State Building or the Statue of Liberty."

"I've been to the Empire State Building," she countered as she stepped onto the elevator ahead of him. She didn't add that she had been around five years old at the time.

Josh moved closer to her as the doors shut. The space was crowded with tourists. She tried not to notice how close he was, or the rays of pleasure that seemed to generate from that closeness.

"How about the Statue of Liberty?" he wanted to know, his breath tickling her ear.

Goose bumps insisted on forming again. She stared straight ahead. "I take the Fifth."

Shannon felt more than heard his laugh. Turning, she saw him wink again. Because that caused a second, strong ripple in her stomach, which she silently told herself was due to the altitude and not his proximity, she turned forward again.

It didn't help check the ripple when he brought his head down again and whispered in her ear, "Caught you."

The sharp intake of breath occurred before she could harness it.

"Something wrong?" he asked.

Yes, something was wrong, Shannon thought. Very wrong. She shouldn't be here with another man, even a harmless one from her past. Certainly not having this strange, strong—okay, romantic—reaction to him.

Now that she thought about it, she wasn't a hundred-percent sure just how harmless Josh McClintock actually was. Joshua McClintock had been, but that was years back. This new, improved version, this "Josh," well, she wasn't so sure about things. Because if he was harmless, then why was she having these feelings and reacting this way to him?

The elevator brought them to the top of the venerable structure and suddenly she was looking at all of Paris, laid out before her like a feast for the eyes. She couldn't contain the excitement she felt.

Or was that Josh creating these feelings within her? She looked at him in wonder.

"What is it?"

She shook her head and looked away again. "Nothing. It's just so beautiful," she murmured.

"Yes," he said softly, looking at her. "I know."

A need for self-preservation and to keep things the

way they were supposed to be had Shannon backing away from Josh and pulling out her cell phone.

"Something wrong?" Josh asked.

"I need to make a call," she told him, a sense of urgency overtaking her. Maybe if she heard Robert's voice, then these strange feelings undulating through her would stop.

Josh nodded, moving away to give her privacy. "I'll be right here, drinking in the sights." He purposely turned away from her, looking down on a city that had begun to court twilight in earnest.

Her fingers almost felt as if they belonged to someone else as she tapped the keypad, hitting the familiar cell number. The phone on the other end began to ring. Mentally, she counted off four rings before she heard a pickup.

Because she knew that her fiancé hated to waste time on the phone, Shannon began to talk fast. "Robert, this is—"

Before she could finish, the answering machine message came on. She heard his stern, no-nonsense voice—a voice she'd once found powerful and strong—but now just found that it separated him from her.

"You've reached the cell phone of Robert Newhall. I can't answer right now, but leave a message and I'll try to get back to you."

She sighed. The operative word here, obviously was "try." She'd been in Paris for more than five hours now and this was her second attempt to reach Robert. Neither try had been successful.

Still, she left another message. "It's Shannon again. Just wanted you to know that I landed safely—" *if you care* "—and that I miss you."

The last phrase was not said all that convincingly, she thought as she snapped her phone shut and dropped it into her pocket.

There was a six-hour difference between Paris and New York. Robert, undoubtedly, was still working, she told herself. He hated being interrupted when he was working. But he'd call her later, she told herself, when he was free.

"Calling the inn to see how Alexis is holding up?" Josh asked pleasantly when she returned to his side.

The question made her feel guilty. She should be concerned with Alexis, not Robert. She'd left Robert working—his favorite state of being. More than likely, he'd hardly notice she was gone. She was supposed to be lending Alexis her support.

Shannon shook her head. "No, I wasn't calling Alexis," she told him.

Josh paused for a moment, observing her. And then he guessed, "He's not there?"

Startled, she looked at him, clearly confused. "How did you—?"

"You look disappointed," he told her.

That was the word for it, she supposed. Disappointed. Because she hadn't reached Robert. "Nothing I'm not used to."

"Being disappointed?" Slipping his arm around her, he guided her back to the elevator. She looked like she needed to eat more than she needed the view, he thought. There were two restaurants housed in the Eiffel Tower, one on the first floor and one, Le Jules Verne, on the second. Since he was partial to Verne's novels, he chose the latter. "You're too young to be disappointed yet," he told her as they rode down to the next level.

"No, I didn't mean disappointed," Shannon quickly amended. *Didn't you?* a voice inside her asked. She deliberately ignored it. She simply missed Robert, that was all. "I mean I'm used to playing phone tag with him. We're both lawyers and between our caseloads, sometimes it's hard for us to connect."

At the restaurant, Josh held up two fingers for the maître d'. The man nodded and took them to a table for two. As they sat down, Josh's eyes never left her. "If you were my fiancée, I'd make time to connect," he assured her.

When a waiter appeared, Josh ordered two glasses of red wine. Shannon waited for the waiter to retreat, then said, "When did you learn all the right things to say?"

Practice, Josh thought, although with Shannon conversation was easy. Maybe because in his mind, hers was the face he'd envisioned every time he'd practiced. With a small laugh, he said, "Came with the growth spurt."

He said it so casually, so unselfconsciously, it made her wonder if his former state had ever bothered him. He seemed completely at ease with himself, she noted. It was a pleasant change from Robert's intensity.

The moment she thought that, she felt guilty again.

"You were short," she agreed, laughing softly, the way a person did remembering a time they enjoyed reliving. And she had loved high school and college. It was just lately she felt as if the fun, the joy, had been drained out of her, as if having fun was just too frivolous for her to contemplate at this stage of her life.

Sitting back in his chair, Josh raised his wineglass to his lips, observing her over the rim. "Tell me, with all this nonconnecting going on, how did you and your fiancé ever happen to hook up?"

It seemed so long ago now, not the three years it actually was. "We clerked for the same judge. Robert was different, then," she said, then shrugged. "Or maybe I was." And had settled for less. Had she settled? She felt confused and this wine had one hell of a kick to it, she thought. "He seemed so dedicated."

Dedicated seemed like a poor word to justify attraction, Josh thought. "So's a word processor, but I wouldn't get engaged to one." A warning look slipped into Shannon's eyes and Josh knew he'd gone a step too far. So he apologized. "Sorry, none of my business." He paused to allow his apology to sink in, sipping his wine as he did so. "So, I hear this was a lifelong dream of your sister's to get married. Paris in the spring."

Shannon was grateful for the change in topic and quickly seized it. "Yes, it is." She thought about how lucky Alexis was. "Gabe's a really nice guy to go along with all this."

Josh smiled. That, he thought, was an understatement. "He's crazy about Alexis. If she wanted a slice of the moon, he'd try to book a flight on the next space shuttle to get it for her. Must be nice to love someone so much."

Shannon sighed softly as she absently took a sip from her own glass. She felt a little fuzzy—and very, very lonely. There was a hole growing inside her that she didn't know what to do with. "Must be."

"Strange words coming from a woman who's engaged," Josh observed.

He'd started out intent on seducing her. When had he gotten caught up in her life? And where had this indignation about her fiancé's apparent lack of feeling come from? Why was he feeling so angry on Shannon's behalf?

"Isn't Robert crazy about you?" Josh asked.

"Robert loves me," Shannon protested quickly, maybe too quickly. Feeling slightly chagrined, she shrugged and said, "Crazy about me? I don't think Robert's actually capable of being crazy about anyone."

Not good enough, Josh thought. Out loud, he said, "He should be." She raised her eyes to his and he saw the surprise there. "You deserve it."

Shannon felt her heart stop beating. And then she felt it go into triple time, racing toward some invisible finish line.

Reaching across the tiny table, Josh placed his hand over hers. "You deserve to have someone crazy about you, Shannon."

One minute they were talking and she was about to protest the very negative picture of Robert that Josh was obviously forming in his mind, the next, they weren't talking at all. They were kissing.

Shannon had never been a shrinking violet. She'd dated extensively in high school and then in college. She was no stranger to the pleasures that a relationship could bring. But this was like standing in a pool of water with lightning striking. Her whole body felt as if it was on the receiving end of an electrical storm.

A hunger sprang up within her that scared her down to the tips of her open-toed shoes.

The desire to stand up, to feel Josh's hard body against hers, was nearly overwhelming. She felt as if she was coming apart at the seams.

Alarms.

She heard alarms.

Alarms were going off in her head. No, wait, they were going off outside her head. On the street below. Sirens. Startled, she pulled her head back and dragged in as much air as she could. She was grateful that she wasn't standing, because she had the feeling that, without support, she would have instantly sunk to the floor.

The sirens were still blaring, getting louder. She looked at Josh in confusion. "Do you hear that?"

He nodded, feeling a bit breathless. Kissing Shannon, he thought, was every bit as wondrous as he'd always imagined it would be. "I guess they have fires here in Paris, too," he told her.

"Fires?" Why did her brain feel so numb? Why wasn't she processing anything he was saying? She'd never felt like this when Robert kissed her. My God, she'd never even felt like this when Robert made love to her.

This was bad, she thought. Very bad.

The waiter came with their meals and she took the moment to try to pull herself together. As if that was possible, she mocked herself. But she had to try. More than that, she had to execute damage control.

As the waiter retreated, Shannon turned toward Josh. Although she wanted to pretend nothing had happened, she had to deal with this before it got completely out of hand. Before he kissed her again and made her forget all her good intentions. She didn't want him getting the wrong idea.

Or, in this case, her mind mocked, the right one. Oh Lord, was she in trouble.

"That wasn't supposed to happen," she told him quietly.

He raised his eyes to hers and, suddenly, her stomach felt like a washing machine in the spin cycle.

"Oh?" The single word seemed to call her on her lie. Or was that just her conscience flaring up?

She pressed her lips together. "I'm a little overwrought, a little up in the air. I think I still have a touch of jet lag and, well, the view up here kind of overwhelmed me…." Her voice trailed off as she silently begged him to understand.

"In other words, you're not quite yourself?" he suggested.

She grabbed at the excuse. "Right."

"All right." Josh nodded complacently. "Then it didn't happen," he told her kindly.

It was what she wanted to hear.

And yet…

Oh, God, she couldn't remember when she felt this confused, this unsure of herself. "Stop being so nice," she told him. His being like this just made everything that much more difficult for her to set right. And made Robert suffer by comparison.

What comparison? she demanded silently. She wasn't out shopping, deciding which vehicle to purchase. She'd made her decision. Robert's ring was on her finger, for heaven's sake. Why was she waffling?

Josh grinned at her. "Somehow, hitting you upside the head doesn't quite seem the way to go to me."

Shannon sighed, closing her eyes for a second. When she opened them again, he was still looking at her. And she felt another strong, almost irresistible urge to kiss him. She put all her energy toward squelching it. "Look, I'm just confused right now."

"Welcome to the club," Josh responded. He was only half kidding when he said it.

THE FOLLOWING TWO DAYS, in between unsuccessful attempts to reach Robert, Shannon did her best to lose herself in all the details involved in pulling together Alexis's wedding and making it everything her sister had ever dreamed of. And in so doing, she tried very hard to forget the effect of that kiss with Josh at the Eiffel Tower. Although the basic groundwork for the wedding had been put down and arranged by her mother's wonderful and energetic Great-Aunt Celeste, there were so many tiny details to see to.

It seemed to Shannon, on the afternoon of their third day in Paris, that one minicrisis after another kept erupting. Alexis seemed to marshal through it all, but Shannon could tell that her sister's nerves were beginning to erode. Shannon did her best to prevent that, to meet every emergency as it came up.

However, she found her patience and her ability to always take the high road and find the positive side to everything severely challenged. And it was no small wonder. The pastry chief, Hugh Gautier, who had been flown in at her father's expense to create the wedding cake, was clashing with Giselle, the chef d'hôtel at Milles Fleurs, who ordinarily ran the inn's kitchen. The menu for the wedding reception was seriously in jeopardy.

As was the entertainment for the event. It seemed that the band that had been flown from New York to Paris to play at Alexis and Gabe's wedding had all come down with some mysterious malady that involved spots and close proximity to a bathroom. They were currently in quarantine.

"I have a very splendid record collection," Great-Aunt Celeste volunteered when apprised of this latest disaster looming over Alexis's wedding. She and the bridesmaids, as well as the mother of the groom, were all gathered in the inn's homey sitting room. All male influence was currently banned. "If you promise to be very careful of them," Celeste said to Alexis, "I can have someone bring my Victrola to the reception."

Taylor, currently standing behind the impeccably dressed white-haired woman, looked at

Shannon and then rolled her eyes heavenward. Alexis covered her face with her hands, turned her body in toward Shannon and quietly sobbed.

"I think she was hoping for live music," Shannon explained to the older woman.

Celeste spread her delicate hands in a gesture that said the explanation made no sense to her. "Music is always alive. It moves. That is what makes it music." Her smile brightened as she looked past Shannon and toward the doorway. "Is that not so?"

"Absolutely."

Shannon turned to see that Josh was standing there. How long had he been there? And why did that even matter to her? Without thinking, her hand went to her hair, smoothing down rebellious waves that had insisted on forming the instant she'd stepped off the plane. But Josh wasn't looking at her. He was looking at Celeste, and then at Alexis.

"Zack, Antonio and Mario play guitar," he told the distraught bride-to-be as he took a couple of tentative steps into the all-female gathering. He glanced at Gabe's mother, and the groom's sisters, Gina, Brigette, Sophia and Annette, for confirmation. All four nodded. "Angelo plays drums and the *other* Angelo plays a keyboard."

"Do they play well, or do they just dabble?" Shannon asked.

Her question was prompted by her experience

with Taylor. Her younger sister, over the course of several years, had gone through a number of instruments, swearing that she would take lessons faithfully only to quickly lose interest and move on to something else. There were five different instruments in their basement, including a tuba, to testify to Taylor's fickleness.

"They're pretty damn good." His eyes darted over to the oldest woman in the room. He flashed her an engaging smile. "Sorry."

Celeste waved her hand and made a dismissive noise. "I have heard much worse, young man." Making her way over to Josh, Celeste hooked both her arms through his, smiling up at him radiantly. "These young men you have just mentioned, they can play for Alexis's wedding?"

Josh knew for a fact that, if asked, all five men would jump at the chance. They practiced together with dreams of becoming an actual band someday.

"I'll go talk to them," he volunteered, then stopped and looked at Alexis. "If it's all right with you."

"*Wishes* is in quarantine," Alexis cried, referring to the whimsical name of the band her father had hired for the occasion. "So, yes, it's all right with me." She smiled at him gratefully. "It's terrific with me," she corrected.

"Great. I'm sure they'd love a chance to ride to the rescue and help you and Gabe out," he told Alexis. Just before he left the room, he glanced at Shannon.

Great-Aunt Celeste moved closer to her. "Perhaps he will need some help persuading these young men," Celeste suggested.

The look in Celeste's eyes said something entirely different as she motioned for her to go after Josh.

Shannon debated for a minute, then gave in. She hurried after Josh.

For the past two days, right after they'd returned from the Eiffel Tower, she'd purposely been avoiding him. But in light of what he'd just done, she felt the need to thank him. Not to say anything to him seemed only rude.

At least, that was the excuse she gave herself.

"You make a habit of that?" Shannon asked, calling after him.

Josh stopped short of the staircase. "A habit of what?"

"Of riding to the rescue."

His grin was hopelessly engaging. She gave up trying to resist or ignore it.

"Whenever possible," Josh said. "Unless my horse is in the stable."

She came up next to him. "I just wanted to add my thanks to Alexis's. I—we," she corrected herself, "really appreciate this. If you hadn't suggested using Gabe's cousins, I don't know where we'd find a band for the wedding."

Josh shrugged off her gratitude. "No thanks

needed. Besides, Alexis is almost family." He saw the puzzled look on her face. "Gabe's like the brother I never had."

"That's right, you were an only child," she said, remembering a conversation they'd had when he tutored her.

His grin widened. "You remembered."

She nodded. "I envied you being an only child. Especially whenever I had to give in to my sisters."

"It's worth the trade-off," he told her earnestly. "Being an only child can be pretty lonely sometimes."

"You don't seem like the type to be lonely."

He looked at her for a long moment. "I was. Then."

Shannon wondered if she was going slightly crazy. She could almost swear that she was being caressed by the word.

The way he said it told her he was no longer lonely. And that she might be the reason for the change. Happiness and an edgy panic flashed through her at exactly the same time.

CHAPTER FOUR

THE FIVE FELLINI COUSINS, when finally tracked down and asked, were more than happy to help out Gabe and his future wife when they learned that the original band was in quarantine. Instantly, guitars were produced while the two Angelos, armed with an English/French dictionary, went in search of a keyboard and a drum set to round out the band. Shannon left one of the three remaining cousins with a list of songs that were to be played at the reception.

"One crisis down, seven hundred and thirty-seven to go," Shannon murmured as she and Josh left the cousins' room.

Josh followed behind her down the stairs. "That many, huh?"

"All right, maybe just seven hundred and twenty-nine," she amended with a smile. "At least, right now it seems like that."

"I think Alexis is very lucky to have someone like you to help handle things for her."

Shannon stopped at the bottom of the stairs and

turned around to face him. He was being so damn nice about everything, it made her feel even guiltier about going to such great lengths to avoid him these past few days. Robert wouldn't have been nearly as nice or helpful, she caught herself thinking. Unless Robert wasn't able to get through—which she doubted—he hadn't even tried to call her back yet.

She'd gone clear across the ocean to France. If she hadn't left a message on Robert's cell phone— several messages—he wouldn't have even known whether or not she had arrived safely.

She could almost hear his voice refuting that: *Use your head, Shannon. If anything had happened, I would have heard it on the news.*

Logical, always logical. She'd found that reassuring once. The stability, after the chaos of her own family and her parents' impending divorce, had been comforting. Now, she wasn't all that sure.

"Look," she said suddenly. "I haven't been avoiding you." Okay, so it was a lie, but just a little white one to spare feelings and involved explanations. "It's just that things have been so crazy."

Joshua nodded, his expression unreadable. "I understand."

Damn it, he was being too nice again. "Okay, I have been avoiding you."

His smile told her that she'd been forgiven before she'd ever said a word.

"Because things have been so crazy?" He repeated her phrase, except that when he said it, there was a whole different meaning to the words, a private one that had nothing to do with the wedding and everything to do with the turmoil their one kiss had generated between them. Or at least, inside her.

"Yes," she said quietly. She looked down at her ring, turning it nervously. Taking a deep breath, she said, "I'm engaged."

"Yes, I know." Slipping his arm around her waist, he moved her out of the way a second before three of Gabe's nephews came barreling down the stairs, racing for the front door.

She looked up at Josh, searching for something, but she didn't know what. Acceptance? Validation? Something to sweep her off her feet to end this agonizing vacillation? Something to help her stick to the promise implied by the engagement ring? "And I love Robert."

"No point in being engaged if you didn't," he agreed amicably.

They moved to an alcove behind the stairs, out of everyone's way. It felt achingly intimate in that tiny space. Shannon sighed, shaking her head. "Why do your agreements sound like points to debate?"

Josh grinned. "I'm from New York, it's in the voice." His eyes were kind when he looked at her.

Kind and wildly stirring. She felt herself reacting. "You were head of the debating team, remember?"

She remembered. She remembered more than that. "And you kept your mouth shut."

Back then, he was always being put down and he had no confidence to stand up for himself. "I was storing up." He didn't like talking about those days and changed the subject. "Look, since you're not avoiding me anymore, how about coming with me to check out a few places?"

Curbing her inclination to say yes immediately, she slid her thumb over the back of her engagement ring, moving the stone forward again. "What kind of places?"

"I'm throwing Gabe a bachelor party tomorrow night and I'm still not sure where to hold it."

She groaned. "Oh, no. I completely forgot about Alexis's bachelorette party."

"Okay, we can make this a double assignment," Josh said. He pulled a rolled-up paperback from his back pocket and held it out to her. "I've got a book here that lists the rowdier nightlife places. And the not-so-rowdy ones," he added.

Shannon could have kissed him—and then reminded herself where that had led the last time she'd gone with impulse. "You really do like to ride to the rescue, don't you?"

Taking her hand, he led the way out the front door. "Whenever possible."

SHANNON SLID bonelessly down into her chair, hardly noticing the charming little outdoor café Josh had brought them to. All she wanted to do was rest.

"Tired?" Josh asked her as he waved over a waitress.

Shannon laughed shortly. She was seven miles beyond tired, past exhausted, on her way to dead.

"I'm not sure if *tired* is the correct word to use right now." She tried to sit up, then decided there was no point to it. She wasn't trying to impress anyone with her good posture. "But I've had my fill of seminaked people for a while."

The waitress stopped short and gave her a deeply quizzical look accompanied by a lopsided smile. Shannon could feel herself blushing. It was getting to be a habit around Josh, she thought.

"She's a recovering voyeur," Josh confided to the young woman, who looked clearly in awe of the information. "I'm her psychiatrist and this is actually quite a breakthrough for her. Two coffees, please," he ordered in the same matter-of-fact tone he'd just used for the diagnosis. He glanced in Shannon's direction to see if she wanted to change her order. When she said nothing, he nodded at the waitress who slowly meandered back into the café's interior.

"Recovering voyeur?" Shannon echoed when she finally found her voice.

If she was expecting Josh to look contrite, she

was disappointed. He looked as if he was enjoying himself too much.

"The waitress seemed satisfied with that explanation. And I did use the word 'recovering,'" he reminded her with a grin.

Too tired to take exception, Shannon could only laugh. "God, you certainly have changed from that guy I knew who couldn't string two words together."

"I could string them," Josh contradicted mildly, "but it was always long after everyone had walked away. My mind was a lot slower in those days." He shrugged carelessly. "Being a broker toughens you up."

"Apparently," she murmured. She realized she was staring at his physique and the way the light blue pullover shirt seemed to adhere to his biceps and his pectorals. Shannon forced herself to look away.

The waitress returned with their coffees just then and Shannon cradled her cup between her hands, absorbing the warmth in silence, or at least her own silence. The street before them was alive with the noise of life and passing cars.

After a few minutes, Josh asked, "See anything you like?"

The question startled her. She'd been lost in her own thoughts. Thoughts that she was not about to share. Shannon coughed and cleared her throat, then looked in his direction. "Excuse me?"

"The clubs," he explained. "Did any of them strike you as being right for Alexis's bachelorette party?"

"The second place we saw, I suppose. Chez Charles. The restaurant looked nice," she added as an afterthought.

Josh suppressed a laugh, but not his comment. "I don't think that anyone at this party is going to be soaking in the ambience or noticing what color the walls are painted. Or even what's being served—on their plates," he added drolly.

Shannon felt her mouth curving despite herself. The topic wasn't the kind she ordinary discussed with a man, not even Robert. Yet somehow, she felt strangely comfortable with the man she was sitting across from. Which seemed odd since, apart from a stack of shared precalculus papers and a handful of quizzes and tests he'd helped coach her through, she and Josh were relative strangers.

She looked down at her coffee. "No, I guess you have a point."

"Let's say I buy you a very late lunch and then we go back and make arrangements?"

Shannon nodded. "Sounds good to me." Especially since it gave her an excuse to spend a little more time with Josh under the guise of helping with Alexis's wedding.

IT WAS ANOTHER TWO HOURS before they finally arrived back at the inn. Rather than go through the sitting area, she and Josh took the back stairs. She didn't want anyone taking note of when she got in or who she'd come in with. Everything, she insisted to herself, was perfectly innocent, but that wouldn't stop Taylor from asking questions or Great-Aunt Celeste, who saw romance everywhere, from giving her a knowing smile.

The last thing she wanted aimed in her direction was a knowing smile.

"See you later," Josh said, walking her to her door. He resisted the temptation to kiss her, a temptation that he noted was unnervingly strong. He backed away as she closed the door.

And he nearly collided with Gabe.

"Was that Shannon I just saw you with?" Gabe asked.

Josh grinned. "Well, at least you don't need glasses yet."

Gabe did not return his grin. "You're not...?" His voice trailed off, as if he was afraid to form the second half of the question.

Josh knew what he was asking. "No." And then, because they were friends and he'd always been honest with Gabe, he added, "Not yet."

Gabe stiffened. "Not ever," he emphasized, like a man envisioning disaster. "And especially not during this trip." He squared his shoulders. "Or I'll have to kill you."

"For doing what comes naturally?" Josh asked

innocently. He made it a rule never to force himself on anyone, never go where he wasn't welcome, but there were definite welcoming vibes coming from Shannon and since she was the girl of his dreams, or had been once, he meant to avail himself of that unspoken invitation.

Gabe pulled him over to the side where, hopefully, they wouldn't be overheard.

"I mean it, Josh. Shannon's off-limits. She's engaged, she's Alexis's sister and on top of that, she's a damn nice person."

"I'm aware of all of the above," Josh informed him. He reclaimed his shirt, drawing it out of Gabe's fingers. "Especially the last part."

Gabe looked at him, exasperated. "So, if she's so nice, why would you want to take her to bed?"

Josh did his best not to laugh. "Did you just hear yourself?"

"You know what I mean. She's too nice a person for you to mess with and do your usual number on."

Josh's eyes were unreadable. "Maybe I won't do my usual number."

Gabe wished he could believe that. There wasn't a woman alive who could get Josh to give up his wandering ways. "Stay away from Shannon," Gabe repeated.

Josh saluted. "Message received, sir." He slipped an arm around his friend's shoulders. "Now, let's talk about your one last fling before you have to lock up your manhood forever."

Gabe did not like the inference. "It's a wedding, not a jail sentence."

Josh shrugged. "Same thing." But this time, he said it with far less feeling than he normally did.

The change in tone was not wasted on Gabe.

THE MEN WERE ALL GORGEOUS.

As Shannon sat, listening to the women around her howl and cheer and applaud wildly, Shannon could truthfully say she had never seen such muscles, such abs, such incredibly slim, perfect hips. But the sum total of all these perfect attributes left her completely bored.

While it was true that the men who were dancing for her sister and the other female members of the Donovan-Fellini wedding party could have easily stepped off a movie set or out of some catalogue dedicated to showcasing absolutely perfect specimens of manhood, she had no doubt that each and every one of these men were about as three-dimensional as used carbon paper. There didn't seem to be a thimbleful of personality among them.

As the music swelled, Shannon's mind drifted elsewhere. She caught herself thinking about Josh, wondering if he was nearly as bored and distracted at Gabe's bachelor party as she was at Alexis's bachelorette party.

Probably not, she mused. Men were men. They liked looking at perfect bare flesh. Well, she needed more. She needed substance. Muscles alone had never been a turn-on. She admired brains, a heart. Kindness. *Then* a man could be cute.

A package deal, she supposed.

She just missed Robert, Shannon insisted silently. That was what was wrong with her.

Excusing herself, Shannon got up and slipped out of the main room.

Leaving the noise behind, Shannon walked into the pink-tiled ladies' room and took out her cell phone. A sigh escaped as she looked at it. Almost five days in Paris and she had yet to connect with Robert. But it was the middle of the night in New York City now and she knew for a fact that Robert did sleep.

Dialing his home phone number, Shannon leaned back against the marble sink and waited as she counted off the number of rings, her stomach tightening with each one.

The instant she heard the receiver on the other end being picked up, she snapped to attention. Her hand tightened around her phone. "Hello?" she said eagerly.

"Hello?" a sleepy voice echoed back at her. "Who's this?"

The voice that answered her call was female. A sleepy female.

What was a sleepy female doing in Robert's apartment? He had no sisters and his mother had died just before they began dating almost three years ago.

Shannon felt numb inside.

"Who's *this?*" she heard herself demanding.

"Tiffany," the voice that was shattering her life into tiny pieces whispered in response.

Shannon took a breath, refusing to let her imagination run away with her. Refusing to believe this was what it sounded like—that Robert was taking advantage of her being out of town. Just as she had secretly suspected.

Damn.

"Is Robert there?" Shannon asked.

"Sure he's here. It's his place," the grating voice whispered. "But he's sleeping. Finally." A squeaky giggle followed, leaving the word *finally* open to all sorts of interpretation, none of which seemed favorable. "Can I take a message?"

This had to be a wrong number. Robert was a common name. She'd hit the wrong number and somehow gotten connected to another Robert. "Robert Newhall," Shannon said, praying the woman on the other line would tell her there was no one there by that name. "I'm looking for Robert Newhall."

Now the whisper took on a layer of impatience. "I told you, he's asleep. Damn near wore both of us out. Now, do you want to leave a message or not?"

"Yes. Tell him that Shannon said to go to hell. It's over."

Shannon didn't remember closing the phone and disconnecting the call. She didn't remember stumbling outside the club or hailing a taxi.

The ride back to the inn was a complete blur.

The only thing she was aware of was the huge ache inside her chest and the word *fool* echoing over and over again in her brain.

A block away from the inn, she realized that she was crying. That she'd been crying ever since she ran out of the club.

The taxi stopped moving. They'd reached the inn. Her driver was looking at her with compassion.

"You will find someone else," he assured her kindly. And then, as she began to deny that she was crying over a man, he added, "Tears, they are always about love."

She pressed her lips together, knowing that to speak would leave herself open to crying again. So instead of saying anything, she handed him a fistful of bills and hurried out of the cab. She felt weak. Dizzy. Stupid.

Squaring her shoulders, she made her way not to the inn, but around back to where the garden had retreated into the darkness. Most everyone was still either at one club or another, but she didn't want to take a chance on running into anyone, not even one of the inn's staff.

She wanted to be alone.

Sitting down on the edge of the fountain, she

wiped away her tears with the heel of her hand. She should have seen it coming, she really should have, Shannon upbraided herself. Robert had been growing more and more distant, more and more wrapped up in his work. Or so he told her. Obviously, whatever he needed, she couldn't give him.

She'd made herself over into a pretzel for the man and he still wasn't satisfied.

Damn him.

How the hell was she going to face everyone? She couldn't stand to see pity in their eyes. When her parents found out about Robert's infidelity, her father would give her a speech, saying that Robert wasn't good enough for her. While she might agree with him, she really didn't want to hear it right now. And her mother would offer to do a number on Robert. Of her two parents, her father might be the ex-sports jock, but it was her mother who was the physical one, highly protective of her own.

Well, *she* could protect herself.

Standing up, Shannon took off her engagement ring and flung it into the center of the fountain.

"Did you remember to make a wish?"

Startled, she swung around to find Josh standing behind her. "What are you doing here? Why aren't you at the bachelor party?"

"One of the guys got sick. Someone had to bring him back to the inn," he said simply. He took a step closer to her, peering at her face. The light here was bad, but even so, he could see the tear stains on her cheek. "Why aren't you with the others?"

She shrugged, looking away. "Naked men bore me."

"Well, we have that in common. Although, I have to say that from where I'm standing, that's not exactly encouraging news." Very gently, he put his fingers beneath her chin and raised her head until her eyes were on his. He suddenly felt very protective, felt the need to take her in his arms and make her tears go away. His voice became serious. "What's wrong?"

Something leaped up inside her. Her heart, she presumed. Obviously, it hadn't turned to ashes the way she'd thought, but was now beating wildly in her throat, sending out all sorts of vibrations through her.

She didn't answer him. Instead, Shannon grabbed hold of his shirt lapel, drew herself up on her toes and sealed her mouth to his.

The fireworks were instantaneous, exploding inside her as the kiss she initiated deepened. Her head began to swirl and she felt almost dizzy, but rather than pull back, to assess, to regroup, she let herself go completely.

Her arms threaded around Josh's neck, she cleaved her body to his, causing the sizzle she felt through her body to grow and become a full-fledged fire within seconds of its inception.

"Take me to your room," she breathed.

Damn it, this was what he'd been waiting for, thinking about. Maybe even subconsciously dreaming about for years. And yet, it seemed wrong somehow, he thought, as if he was taking advantage of her. Suddenly, he was thinking beyond the moment, beyond the desire. Thinking only of the sad-eyed woman before him.

`He didn't want anything that might happen between them to be marred by her regrets. So he drew back and looked at her. "Shannon, are you sure?"

Why was he arguing with her? Why wasn't he just sweeping her off her feet the way she wanted? The way she needed? "Take me to your room, or a broom closet if that's too full. Or right here."

As she said it, she moved against him, causing all sorts of delicious sensations to go shooting through his loins.

Damn, but she was a handful. "Shannon, what happened?" he wanted to know.

The concern in his voice did her in.

If he'd jumped at what she was offering, then maybe she could have backed away at the last minute, sought her senses from somewhere. But Josh was obviously thinking of her, maybe even feeling her pain somehow. All she knew was that Josh was being thoughtful and possessed the greatest set of lips she'd ever encountered.

Robert could boast of neither trait.

It was the last time she thought of Robert for the next eight hours.

CHAPTER FIVE

BECAUSE SELFLESSNESS only went so far, Josh gave up trying to reason her out of doing what they both wanted. When he brought her to his room, it was empty, as he knew it would be. The moment the door closed, shutting out the rest of the world, they came together and almost from the first, a strange feeling of homecoming descended over him.

Something happened.

Josh had always enjoyed the women he'd made love with. It was always a mutually shared, satisfying experience. But it involved merely the joining of two bodies and the physical reactions that joining generated. It never went any further, which was the way he wanted it, the way he expected it to be.

There was something more at play this time around, something deeper. Something that made him hold back, go slower and absorb every caress, every tentative exploration, every wild, heart-pounding surge that occurred.

He'd never been one in search of his own

pleasure to the exclusion of his partner. That road held no allure for him, but this time, with Shannon, her pleasure, her enjoyment, her responses took complete precedence over his own.

They *made* his own responses come into being.

And when it was over, when he lay exhausted beside her, Josh caught himself wanting to go back to the start and begin all over again.

And again.

Until he was completely spent. And even then, when it was done and he could hardly breathe he was so tired, it was still different.

The restlessness didn't come.

The restlessness that always fueled his desire to move on. To get up and leave the woman and the interlude because it was in the past and had no claim to him or to the present.

With Shannon, all he wanted to do was hold her in his arms, smell her hair, feel the warmth of her skin as she curled into him. He felt like a runner who had finally crossed the finish line. Who'd made it home.

He wanted to linger.

It was, he realized, as if she'd single-handedly, and without knowing it, torn him down and rebuilt him in the space of one wild, passion-filled night. He'd always wanted her and now he had her—and he wasn't disappointed.

Moonlight was streaming in through the window

he'd forgotten to close. He even heard crickets. The chirping noise meant the crickets were looking for one another, searching for their soul mate.

Maybe he was one up on them. It made him smile.

Josh felt Shannon stirring against him. She sighed, her warm breath rippling along his skin and making something in his belly tighten as a fresh wave of desire came out of nowhere to find him. To urge him on.

The woman made him want to leap tall buildings in a single bound.

Tightening his arm around her, Josh looked down at the face he knew in his heart had been the only one he'd ever wanted to see beside him as dawn nudged aside the layers of the night.

He kissed the top of her head and realized that he had never done that before, never been moved by tenderness to share a moment. This, he thought, was a whole new experience for him. It was a little scary, but he liked it. Really liked it.

"Something wrong?" he asked her.

No, she thought, everything was right. For the first time in a long time, everything felt right. Absolutely right. There was no tension in her body, no tight shoulders shooting pains up to her neck. No anxiety humming along the perimeter of her mind as she wondered if she'd said something that Robert would disapprove of.

She felt, she realized, like herself again. Her old self.

Shifting, she turned into him. "I was just wondering where your roommates were."

"If they're not passed out in the club, they're probably off somewhere practicing." She looked at him, confused. He smoothed out the single furrow in her brow. "They're part of Alexis and Gabe's band, remember?"

That's right, the two Angelos. She and Josh had come to his room the other day looking for Gabe's cousins. She smiled. "Very clever of you."

He wasn't following her. "Clever?"

Shannon's smile widened. "Getting rid of any witnesses."

When he'd suggested using Gabe's cousins, he hadn't thought about them vacating the room. He was just trying to help Alexis. "That wasn't the plan."

Her eyes grew alert. "What was the plan?"

Freudian slip, he thought. He didn't want her to think that he had plotted any of this, even though, at the outset, that had been his intent. It seemed somehow wrong now.

"To come to Paris and stand up for my best friend. And help with the wedding any way I could," he added the last part for good measure.

She hesitated, then shrugged. Sitting up, she drew the sheet around her. "Well, you certainly helped me see the light."

There was a very real temptation to draw her back into his arms and let whatever happened after that happen. But he refrained. She needed to talk, so he urged her on. "And what light would that be?"

Shannon dragged her hand through her hair. Waves of deep strawberry fell about her shoulders. "That I can do better."

He sat up and looked at her. "I can't tell, was that an insult?"

She suddenly realized what that had to sound like to him. "No, not you. God, I didn't mean you. I meant Robert."

"So, it's over?"

"So over it should have never been." Shannon looked down at her hand and remembered the ring she'd flung into the fountain. She knew for a fact—Robert had made a point of telling her—that it was expensive. She still didn't regret throwing it away. Stretching out her fingers, she held out her hand. "It looks better this way. Naked."

Josh grinned, reaching for her again. "The same could be said for you." His lips came down on hers in a slow, deep kiss.

Shannon allowed herself to linger for one long, languid moment, savoring the feel of his lips on hers. But just as she began to sink into the kiss, she forced herself to pull back. If she remained any longer, she wouldn't be able to leave. Or want to.

So she placed her hands on his chest and gently

pushed Josh away. "No, someone's liable to come in. I'd better get back to my room."

His eyes washed over her as she rose from the bed. She took his breath away. That didn't usually happen after lovemaking, only before.

Definitely something different was going on here, he thought, pleased beyond measure. She was everything he always knew she'd be. And more. It was, he realized, as if he'd been waiting for her all his life.

His smile was sensual as he asked, "Want me to help you get dressed?"

Right. She'd never get out that way. "Said the spider to the fly."

"I don't think the spider wanted to dress the fly, but maybe you're right." He sat up, the sheet pooling around his midsection. She had already hurried back into her clothing, much to his regret. And suddenly, the moment turned serious for him. "Listen, I don't want this to be a one-time thing."

She stopped to look into the mirror, vainly attempting to do something with her hair. "You don't have to be gallant."

He laughed shortly as he got up and pulled his trousers on quickly. "Gallant. Now there's a word I don't remember being called. I like it." He heard her laugh and looked over his shoulder. She was crossing to the door. He couldn't read her expression. "Seriously, I want to see you again."

"We're in the same wedding party," she reminded him glibly. No matter what she was feeling about the night they'd just shared, she didn't want to make too much of this. That was what had gotten her in trouble in the first place, letting her feelings run away with her.

"After that," he insisted as he crossed to the door. "I don't want you going back to Robert when he comes crawling to beg you to forgive him and take him back."

Now there was a scenario that was never going to happen. "Robert doesn't crawl."

He feathered his fingers through her hair. That same funny feeling was stirring inside him. "He would if he knew what was good for him."

Josh knew what to say to make her feel special. Shannon paused to kiss him again, then grabbing her shoes, she sailed out the door. "You're a dear," she tossed over her shoulder before shutting the door behind her.

Watching her leave, Josh felt as if he was back in senior year high school all over again. Back in high school and feeling helpless. Except that this time, he intended to do something about it.

"OH MY GOD, were you just in Josh's room?" Alexis demanded, her hands on her hips, her eyes registering complete shock.

Damn.

Walking into the hall without first looking, Shannon had all but backed into her sister. Sneaking around was just not her forte, Shannon thought.

She decided to brazen it out. "Looks that way, doesn't it?"

Alexis looked as if her world had just been shattered. "But you're engaged—to Robert."

Shannon held up her left hand and wiggled her empty ring finger. "Not anymore."

Alexis looked at the finger, stunned. "Because you slept with Josh?" She grabbed both of Shannon's arms, as if she was going to shake some sense into her. "Shan, do you know how many women he goes through in a year?"

Shannon wasn't ready to come off her cloud, not yet. "I'm not interested in those statistics."

"Well, you're going to hear them," Alexis insisted. "Gabe told me Josh likes to set his sights on a girl and see how long it takes him to wear her down. The more challenging the conquest, the better, although most women don't even try to resist him." Releasing her sister, Alexis waved her hands helplessly in the air. Alexis was exaggerating but she felt it was for Shannon's own good. She didn't want to see her sister making a mistake. Paris could turn a girl's head and her heart. And Josh was so much more charming than Robert. "It all has something to do with his being short in high school and making up for lost time. I really didn't pay that much attention to what Gabe said, but I do know Josh isn't the kind of guy who's going to settle down. He said he's not even going to think about that until he's at least forty. He even tried to talk Gabe out of getting married," she finished with indignant umbrage. "And Robert called me," she added triumphantly.

Now that was out of character. Robert rarely had any contact with her family. He claimed she was much too involved with them, that she should "grow up" and break her ties. His attitude bothered her a great deal. "Called you? Why?"

"Because he's trying to reach you and couldn't get through on your cell phone."

There was a reason for that, Shannon thought. She'd turned it off after she'd found out that Robert had taken some bimbo to his bed.

"He sounded really upset," her sister was saying.

Men who got caught, Shannon thought, unmoved, generally were. "I'll talk to him when I'm good and ready," Shannon answered, knowing that wouldn't be for a very long time. "And you, little sister, have too much on your plate to worry about what anyone else is doing—and this means me." She raised her chin. "I can handle my own life just fine, thank you," she concluded, only wishing she was half as certain as she tried to sound.

THE WEDDING CEREMONY was five hours away when Shannon slipped out of the inn and went for a walk. She left without telling anyone, careful to avoid her own family and Gabe.

And especially Josh.

She'd never been a quitter, never run away from anything. Not life, not a challenge, not a fight. But right now, she had to admit she felt like running. Like leaving everything and everyone behind, hailing a cab to the airport and hopping the first flight back to New York. Not to see Robert, God knows. She'd ended that officially over the phone, telling him exactly what she thought and not allowing him a word in edgewise. It had felt wonderful and afterward she'd felt liberated.

Almost as liberated as when she'd made love with Josh.

No, her desire to flee had nothing to do with Robert, or even with throwing herself into her work, her usual cure of choice whenever she needed to keep things at bay until she could handle them. This time she just wanted to get away from the wedding and be by herself to try to sort things out. She was too close to things in the inn.

Too close, she knew, to Josh.

She was clearly rebounding, she insisted silently. And that wasn't fair to Josh. She'd tried to make him understand at the rehearsal dinner last night, but her resolve kept melting whenever she was near him. She needed space.

In her heart of hearts, if she were being honest with herself, she'd known for a while that things between Robert and her weren't going to work out. She'd been too stubborn, too optimistic, to admit the truth.

When she'd fallen for Robert, he'd been a different person. Slowly, he began to change and she began to change with him in order to try to please him. Over the months, she'd tried to make herself over into someone Robert would approve of. But there was always something he found fault with, some minor transgression she'd unwittingly committed which made him frown and made her heart sink. They didn't belong together.

Now that she'd taken the first huge step away, she had to admit that she really didn't like the person Robert wanted her to be. Driven, but without passion, focused, but without joy.

Stopping to smell a wild rose, Shannon closed her eyes. She couldn't remember the last time she and Robert had laughed together. She couldn't live like that.

She *wouldn't* live like that.

She supposed, in a way, she had Josh to thank for her epiphany. Josh had shown her that there was life beyond Robert and for that, womanizer or not, she'd always be grateful to him.

The trouble was, she thought as she slowly began to walk back to the inn and her responsibilities, she was falling in love with Josh. At least Robert had said he wanted to marry her. But Josh?

She had a feeling that Alexis was right. Josh wasn't the marrying kind. Joshua from high school might have been, but this new, improved model with the wicked, wicked mouth wasn't.

Her thoughts were interrupted when Alexis came running down the path to her and grabbed her arms.

"Omigod, Omigod, Omigod," Alexis cried breathlessly, gasping for air.

Now what? This did not look like woman who was about to be married in a few hours. Beset with problems, it looked as if Alexis had finally had her meltdown. Bracing herself, Shannon slowly extracted her arms from her sister's death grip. "What's wrong, Alexis?"

"The cat," Alexis sobbed. Her sister began pulling her back to the inn. "The cat destroyed it."

Okay, Alexis had officially gone over the deep end. This wasn't making any sense. Shannon tried to stop walking, but Alexis wouldn't let her. "What cat, Alex? Destroyed what?"

"The cat that's been lurking around here," Alexis said, and Shannon vaguely recalled seeing a cat darting out of everyone's way a couple of times. She assumed it belonged to the owner of the inn. "It got its claws caught in my veil. My *veil,*

Shannon," she wailed. "I walked into my room and found that creature shredding my veil." Tears were flowing down her perfectly made-up face now. "What am I going to do?"

Entering the inn, Shannon mentally crossed her fingers. It was never as bad as Alexis thought it was. "All right, let's go see the damage."

Following her up the stairs like a distraught puppy, Alexis cried, "There's nothing left."

There was a lot left, most of it completely untouched by furry paws or extended claws. Shannon had a strong suspicion that Alexis had sent the cat scrambling for its life before it had a chance to do any real major damage.

Gingerly picking up the delicate material from the floor where it had fallen, Shannon carefully inspected it. She discovered a total of two small rips, both of which were not located in readily visible areas.

Still holding the veil, she looked at her sister with confidence and smiled. "This can be fixed."

Alexis stared at the veil. "How?" she cried.

Shannon slipped an arm around her sister's slender shoulders and laughed softly. This disaster, at least, was easily remedied. Unlike her own life. "It's called sewing, Alexis."

"But I don't know how to sew," Alexis protested.

"We've got a lot of women in this place. Someone must know how to sew. In a pinch, I can do it," she added. Her stitches weren't the neatest, but they would hold. Alexis was still a ghostly shade of white. "Breathe, Alexis, breathe."

Obediently, Alexis drew air in, then slowly let it out again. She looked at her sister with unabashed relief and gratitude. "Oh, Shannon, I don't know what I'd do without you."

Shannon merely smiled, examining the material again to make sure she hadn't missed another tear. "You'd manage."

Alexis shook her head. "No, really." Wanting to do something for her, Alexis hit on the only thing she could think of. "If you want Josh, you've got him. I'll have Gabe tie him up with a bow for you."

She mustered a smile for Alexis's sake because she knew her sister meant well. "Thank you, Alexis, but I'll do my own shopping for men." Changing the subject, Shannon decided to go in search of Alexis's future mother-in-law. Audrey Fellini liked nothing better than being needed and pitching in. "And don't worry about the veil. Fixing it will be a piece of cake," she assured her just before she left the room.

The color slowly began to return to her sister's face.

"SO THERE YOU ARE," Josh said, coming out to the fountain. After searching the inn, it occurred to him that Shannon might be here, where he had found her the night of the bachelor party. Was she having second thoughts about her terminated engagement? Was she searching in the water for the ring? "I've been looking all over for you."

Dressed and ready, with baby's breath flowers woven through her hair, Shannon had opted for another moment alone to pull herself together before the ceremony began. Since the guests were inside, she came out here where there were only the caterers to deal with.

At the sound of Josh's voice, Shannon looked up and saw him walking toward her. He looked incredibly handsome in his dark tuxedo. It took effort to keep from melting all over again.

She reminded herself of what Alexis had told her. She was only one of Josh's many conquests. She'd thought she was okay with that. Now she knew that she wasn't. But that was her problem, not his.

"Why?" she asked, her voice distant. "Is there another wedding emergency?"

"No, no emergency. I just wanted to see you."

As he took a step toward her, she took one step back, keeping the distance the same. "Look, there's no need to pretend."

Josh looked at her uncertainly. "Pretend?"

"That you're interested in me," she clarified, annoyed that her voice sounded almost squeaky to her ear. Shannon took a breath, reminding herself that she'd vowed to stay cool. "Alex told me all about your MO."

He looked at her blankly, all the while a hint of panic beginning to take hold. He knew in that instant that he didn't want to lose her. Ever. She *was* the woman of his dreams. "My MO?"

Her hold on patience slipped. "Will you stop repeating everything I say?"

"When I stop being mystified by the things you say, I will," he told her simply. "Now, what are you talking about?"

"I'm talking about a man who's made it his life's goal to sleep with every woman he comes across."

Josh pushed his sleeve back from his wrist, looking down at his watch. "Talk fast, Shannon, I'm supposed to make love to Great-Aunt Celeste in five minutes. It's all the time we have before the wedding starts," he deadpanned. Then, pushing his sleeve back into place, he looked at her. "Do you see how dumb that sounds?"

She hadn't *really* meant that he wanted to sleep with *every* woman. Just the ones he considered attractive. She raised her chin defensively. "Doesn't mean it's not true."

"Okay, you got me," he said, raising his hands like a man surrendering. There was a reason, however shallow now that he looked back at it, he'd behaved the way he had. And why he was now ready to turn his back on his former bachelor way of life. "I was the guy everyone either ignored or ridiculed in high school and maybe, when the 'magic fairy' transformed me from a toad to a regular, acceptable guy, I went a little haywire for a while and tried to make up for lost time."

Shannon began to turn away from him, but he couldn't let her. Moving around to face her again, Josh put his hands on her shoulders to anchor her in place. She had to hear him out.

"Looking back, that was dumb. But maybe it happened because the one person I really wanted was never accessible to me."

"And that person was?" she asked.

He couldn't believe she was actually asking. Was she that unaware of the effect she'd always had on him? "Oh, c'mon, Shannon. Were you really that oblivious to me in high school? Was I just this invisible voice to you, the one who helped you through your math tests?"

She stared at him, stunned. "You had a crush on me?"

He snorted. Long-suppressed anger rose to the fore. "It was a hell of a lot more than a crush and maybe, if you hadn't been surrounded by all those athletes, you might have realized that."

She continued to stare at him, utterly dumbfounded. "But you never said anything."

"Because I didn't want you to laugh in my face." It was every teenage boy's nightmare, to be rejected as unworthy of the person he dreamed of every night.

She looked at him for a long moment. Is that

what he actually thought? That she'd laugh at him if he'd asked her out? Shannon suddenly felt hurt and insulted. "I guess you didn't know me at all, did you?"

He looked into her eyes, and saw something that gave him pause. And a glimmer of hope. "You would have gone out with me if I'd asked you? But I was shorter than you."

"I would have worn flats. You were a nice person then."

Damn, when he thought of all the time that had been wasted, all the time he couldn't recapture…

But there was still the future.

"I still am," he assured her. Strains of organ music began to fill the air. The ceremony would be starting soon. "And I'd like to take you out. Officially. The second this wedding is all behind us."

There was something she wanted more, to build a relationship with him. A relationship with a future. Hope began to form within her. "You're not just saying that?"

He took hold of her hands, as if making a pledge. "Yes, I'm saying that. And I'll go on saying that until you finally go out with me."

"Okay." She grinned. "It's a date. The second we step off the plane in New York. Now stop talking," she ordered, winding her arms around his neck.

He slipped his hands around her waist, drawing her closer. "Your every wish is my command."

"I do like the sound of that," she murmured.

"Hopefully, you'll like this even better," he said, just before he kissed her.

PICTURE PERFECT

Cindi Myers

For the ladies at Romancing the Yarn

CHAPTER ONE

Milles Fleurs—six days before the wedding

LACEY JESSUP SLID the baking pan from the oven and bent low over the twin *baguettes* and inhaled deeply. The yeasty aroma of freshly baked bread filled her with a deep contentment. The smell reminded her of the Iowa farmhouse kitchen where she'd spent so many hours growing up. Here in Paris, she could recreate this sense of home anytime she opened a bag of flour. It pleased her to think that bread was much the same, even halfway around the world.

And now, thanks to weeks of work in the classrooms and labs of Le Cordon Bleu and the kitchen here at Milles Fleurs, the inn where she worked, she had finally mastered the art of making the perfect French loaf.

She transferred the *baguettes* to the cooling rack and admired their perfectly browned crusts beneath their dustings of flour, four diagonal slashes evenly spaced across the top of each loaf.

"Very nice, *chérie*," the *chef d'hôtel* at Milles Fleurs, Giselle Fortier, peered over Lacey's shoulder and nodded approvingly. "A little more practice and no one will ever guess the *baguettes* are made by an American."

The qualifier to the praise erased Lacey's smile. "You think I need more practice?" she asked.

"Only a little." Giselle nodded at the loaves. "The shape, it is still a little fat in the middle, *non?* The ideal *baguette* is uniformly long and thin, with no bulges."

Lacey nodded. Now that Giselle had pointed them out, she could see that her *baguettes* did indeed have bulges. "Next time, I'll make them perfectly," she said, moving to the kitchen island to begin preparing vegetables for tomorrow's *quiche lorraine.* Even as she said the words, she could almost hear her mother cautioning her that nothing was ever perfect—no matter how much Lacey wanted it to be so.

It was true that as a child, Lacey had spent hours creating elaborate fantasies in which her life played out like a Hollywood movie: she was the perfectly beautiful star living in the perfectly glamorous house, being courted by the most perfectly handsome man. Though real life seldom measured up to her fantasies, she never abandoned hope.

When she decided to pursue a career as a chef, she'd set her sights on training at Le Cordon

Bleu, the acclaimed Académie D'Art Culinaire with a reputation for exacting standards and five-star elegance.

Now she lived and studied in Paris, the romantic City of Light. Every day she was surrounded by the ultimate in fashion and culture. In her free time she had visited the Louvre, strolled among the flowers at Tuileries and lingered at sidewalk cafés, entertaining herself with daydreams of a torrid love affair with a dashing Frenchman.

So far, no such Frenchman had appeared. They were all apparently pursuing beautiful, elegant Frenchwomen. As for American men, Lacey had made mistakes with them before.

She selected a knife from the wood block beside the worktable and chose an onion to chop, but before she could begin, the door to the kitchen burst open. "What does a man have to do to get something to eat around here?" A tall American man with windblown light brown hair and a slightly ruddy complexion strode into the room. "I've spent all day flying halfway across the world to get here and the woman at the reception desk tells me the dining room is closed."

Lacey stared, wide-eyed. The man filled the room with his larger-than-life presence, as if he'd *personally* flown a plane across the world, at times dodging enemy fire, and perhaps stopping to tame a lion or two along the way.

"There is a café one-half kilometer down the street that will be happy to serve you, I am sure," Giselle said, all warmth gone from her voice.

"After the day I've had, I don't need the hassle of going out to eat." He spotted the cooling *baguettes* and walked over to them. "These smell great. Could I have some of this bread, and maybe some cheese?"

Giselle shook her head and left the room. Though Lacey's French was still rudimentary, she thought the chef muttered something about "rude Americans."

"What's her problem?" the man asked.

Lacey could have told him that if he had asked politely for a *petit repas*—if he had been charming and had flattered Giselle's cooking or praised her beauty—in other words, if he had behaved more as a Frenchman would have—he might have succeeded in talking the chef into preparing him an omelet or a hearty sandwich. But what was the use? American men were not Frenchmen. They were used to getting their way. This one was no exception and she could see he wouldn't take no for an answer.

"I can prepare you some bread and cheese." She moved toward the bread knife in its holder by the wooden breadboard. "And we have some grapes."

"Perfect. I'm starving." He sat on one of the tall stools at the prep counter and watched as she sliced the still-warm bread and arranged it on a plate. His broad shoulders sagged with weariness and a shadow of beard darkened his cheeks and jaw, but there was a nervous energy to him as well, as if he was prepared to leap off the stool at any moment. She added a generous wedge of cheese from beneath the glass dome on the counter, and a bunch of grapes from the cooler. Spying the jug of *vin ordinaire* on the pantry shelf, she hesitated, then brought it to the counter with the plate. "Would you like wine?" she asked.

"That would be great." He plucked a grape from the bunch and popped it into his mouth as she poured the wine. "I don't know why it is you can't get decent food on planes anymore," he said. "They actually ran out of meals on my flight from Frankfurt, and the cardboard they tried to pass off as a sandwich on the leg from Beirut was inedible." He tore off a hunk of bread, added a sliver of cheese, and made a groaning sound as he bit into it.

Lacey bit back a laugh at his theatric enjoyment of the simple bread, cheese and fruit. She had forgotten how demonstrative some American men could be, even with strangers. The Frenchmen she knew were considerably more formal and reserved. "Are you with the wedding party?" she asked. As far as she knew, the entire inn was booked by the Donovan and Fellini families and their many relatives and friends. For the past several days they'd been flying in from all over. All the rooms were full and even the former butler's pantry off the upstairs sitting room had been hastily converted into guest quarters, though there was scarcely room for a narrow bed and chair in the small space.

"Yes, I'm sorry to say I am." He stuck out his hand. She hesitated, then took it. His grip was strong, his palm calloused and warm. "Marc Kendrick," he said. "My cousin is the groom. If I'd gotten to him sooner, I might have talked him out of this foolishness, but I've been out of the country for most of the last year."

"You aren't happy your cousin's getting married?" she asked. The little she'd seen of the bride and groom had led her to believe they were both nice people, and obviously very much in love. So far their families at the inn had gotten along well.

"I guess I don't see what Gabe's hurry is to settle down." Marc took a sip of wine. "He sounded pretty thrilled when I talked to him on the phone, so I guess I'm not *unhappy* for him. This bread's really good, by the way." He tore off another large piece.

"Thank you." He really wasn't rude at all. In fact, he was nice, in a rough sort of way.

"What were you doing in Beirut?" she asked. It seemed an impossibly exotic destination to her. Until her arrival in Paris two months ago, she had never been out of the United States.

"Working," he said. "I didn't want to leave, either, but I let myself get talked into photographing my cousin's wedding." He shook his head. "I tried my best to get out of it. I told him weddings really aren't my thing, but to most people one picture is very much like the next. I make my living with a camera, so they figure I'd be just thrilled to take sappy staged shots of their big day."

"You're a photographer?"

"Photojournalist." He grimaced. "I document the action in war zones and chronicle world tragedies. I *don't* do blushing brides and grinning groomsmen."

She laughed at his obvious distaste. "Sounds like it will be a nice change for you," she said. "All that war and tragedy must get depressing. And what could be more romantic than a wedding in Paris?"

"I'll take a weekend dodging sniper fire in the Gaza Strip over three days in the company of starry-eyed lovers any day," he said.

Harsh words, but Lacey didn't really believe them. Marc Kendrick wore the attitude of the bitter cynic the way an actor wore a costume for a play. But his firm grip when they'd shaken hands and the appreciative way he consumed a simple meal made her think there was more to this disgruntled man than he let the world see. "Lovers can be a bit hard to take when you're lonely yourself," she said.

His gaze locked to hers, intense. She felt as

much as saw the truth of her words in the pain that flashed through his eyes, quickly masked by a cynical sneer. "There's a lot to be said for one's own company," he said. He pushed the empty plate away and stood. "Thanks for the food. You saved me from inflicting my tortured French on some poor waitress."

She watched the kitchen door swing shut behind him, then collected his empty plate and glass and carried them to the deep sink. Of all the men who had arrived for the wedding so far, Marc Kendrick was definitely the most interesting. Certainly the most worldly and cynical, possibly even the most rude and brash. But she held none of that against him. Like Lacey herself, he was in an unfamiliar situation far from his usual home. That he'd allowed her to glimpse the uneasiness behind his bravado touched her. And as out of place as she sometimes felt in the bustle and glamour of Paris, she took a great deal of comfort in knowing that a man accustomed to dodging bullets and escaping disaster in Third World countries could be unnerved by something as wonderful and joy-filled as a wedding.

HIS HUNGER SATED, Marc felt more like himself. Good thing the younger of the two women guarding the kitchen hadn't been as snippy as her coworker. He'd been surprised to find an American wearing the traditional white smock and chef's toque, but he'd been too focused on the excellent bread and cheese she'd served him to inquire as to her background. Now he regretted not finding out her name.

No doubt he'd see her again during the week he was stuck here. If not, it didn't really matter. All he wanted was to take care of this family obligation and get back to his real work.

Focused on his thoughts, he turned a corner in the hallway and almost collided with a smaller man. "Marc! You finally made it. I was beginning to worry!"

"My plane was delayed in Frankfurt." Marc managed a smile for the older man with the elaborate mustache. "It's good to see you again, Uncle Frank."

"It's good to see you, too." The two men embraced, Frank Fellini's arms tight around his nephew, the warmth of the gesture triggering a knot in Marc's chest. Frank had been like a father to him, practically raising him after his real dad ran off.

"Have you just arrived?" Frank asked. "Are you checked in yet?"

"Yes. Though I suspect the room they gave me was formerly a broom closet."

Frank laughed. "It probably was. There are so many of us here, most of the young people are sharing. I hope you don't mind close quarters."

"I've stayed in worse." In Iraq he'd stayed in mud-floored barracks and in Afghanistan he'd slept in caves. At least this time he'd lucked out and didn't have to bunk with anyone else—probably because there wasn't room for another bed in the small space.

Frank stood back. "Let me look at you." He studied Marc and shook his head. "You look worn-out. And you're too thin. You're not taking care of yourself."

"The food in Beirut isn't always the best. And I'm tired from my flight." He smiled again, more touched than annoyed by his uncle's scolding. "I'll be fine once I've had a good night's sleep."

"It's good that you're here," Frank said. "You'll have a few days to relax before the wedding. Eat some good food, drink some wine, see the city." He grinned. "Catch up with family. It'll be a real vacation for you."

He nodded. He couldn't remember when he'd last had a real vacation, and that was fine with him. He wasn't the type who enjoyed idleness, or playing the tourist. "How is Gabe?" he asked. The groom in this wedding was Frank's son.

Frank's grin widened even more, setting the ends of his elaborate mustache—which Marc suspected benefited from a generous application of black dye—to quivering. "Gabe is in love. Very happy. And Alexis, his fiancée, is a wonderful girl.

You'll meet her tomorrow. They're both so excited and grateful that you're going to photograph the wedding for them. It will mean so much more to them, coming from family."

Marc wondered if this was true. Having him here certainly meant a lot to Uncle Frank, who had been the one to ask him to be the wedding photographer. Marc would never have said no to Frank. "I'll do my best," he said. "You know this isn't really my usual kind of work."

"You'll do a great job, I know. I wish your mother could have joined us."

"She sends her love, and she wishes she could have been here, too. Unfortunately, with the new job she couldn't get any vacation time." Marc's mother—Frank's sister—had recently taken a teaching position at a new school.

"I'm happy for her, but we'll miss her. And speaking of the women in your life…" Frank arched one eyebrow. "Is Nancy with you? I was hoping we'd get to see her again."

Inwardly, he cringed at the question he'd known was coming. "Nancy and I split up a couple of months ago." She'd packed her things and moved out of the New York apartment they'd shared while he was on assignment in Korea. They'd been drifting apart for a while, so he hadn't even been all that surprised when she'd called to tell him she was leaving.

Frank's face fell. "I'm so sorry," he said. "She was a nice young woman."

He nodded. "She was." He shrugged. "It's hard to have much of a love life when you travel as much as I do." Or when you weren't the type of man women stuck with. Everyone he'd ever dated had eventually found some reason to leave. He'd decided he wasn't meant for any long-term relationships.

Frank's expression darkened further. "I know how much you love your work, but there are more important things in life than a job. People—and your relationships with them—will mean more to you in the long run than all the prizes and awards you can hang on a wall."

The implied criticism of his lifestyle stung. Did his uncle really think he was so shallow? "I get a lot of satisfaction from my work that goes beyond awards and prizes," he said. "I help make people aware of what's going on in the world. That often results in aid and attention that improves people's lives."

Frank nodded. "Yes, yes, I'm aware of all that. But in the meantime, what are you doing to improve your own life?" He leaned forward and patted Marc's shoulder. "You can't blame me for wanting to see you as happy as Gabe is now."

"I'm happy," he said. Or at least content. "You don't have to worry about me."

"You're right. This week is for celebrating, not

worrying. It's good to have you with us. I'll let you get to bed now."

Right. That's what he needed, a good night's sleep. Then he'd be better prepared to face a week of dealing with romantic sentiments and wedding hysteria. Give him a guerrilla uprising any day!

CHAPTER TWO

"WHAT HAPPENED with that rude American man last night after I left?"

Lacey had scarcely donned her toque the next morning when Giselle fired the question at her. The Frenchwoman's eyes sparked with curiosity as she expertly twisted dough for the morning's croissants.

Lacey pulled a basket of eggs from the cooler and set half a dozen to boil. The rest would go into omelets. Though the French rarely ate more than croissants and coffee for breakfast, in deference to the American appetites of its guests, the inn offered a full breakfast. "I gave him some bread and cheese. He really wasn't that rude, just hungry and tired."

"Bah! Just a typical man, then." Giselle pinched off a hunk of dough and rolled it between her hands. "But a handsome one, *non?*"

"Yes, he was handsome." A warm shiver danced through her at the memory of Marc Kendrick's hand wrapped around hers. Not that it meant anything but that she hadn't been that close to a man in months. "There are a lot of handsome men here for the wedding." Marc's cousin, the groom, Gabe Fellini and the best man, Josh McClintock, were both very good-looking young men, though they lacked the intensity of Marc.

"Then you are a lucky young woman, indeed," Giselle said. "To be working in a house full of handsome, single men, surrounded by the romance of an upcoming marriage. Unless, of course—" she slid a sideways glance at Lacey "—you already have a lover."

Lacey shook her head. "No."

"And no one is waiting for you back home in America?"

"No. No one is waiting for me." So far she had not exactly been a femme fatale when it came to men. She had a habit of getting starry-eyed over men who were all wrong for her. Shortly before coming to Paris, she'd been dumped by the owner of the restaurant where she worked. Her mother had warned her early on that they had nothing in common and it would never work, but Lacey had never let logic stop her from falling for a man. But once again, her mother had been right. Raul had dropped her in favor of a woman he met at his country club.

When she'd been accepted at Le Cordon Bleu, she'd dreamed of meeting a dashing Frenchman who would sweep her off her feet, but she might as well have been invisible for all the local men noticed her.

"Perhaps you will make a conquest during this wedding party," Giselle said. She arranged the last croissant on the baking tray and began brushing the pastries with butter.

Lacey laughed. "I doubt it. It's hard for someone like me to compete with you sophisticated Frenchwomen." So far the only man who'd paid any attention to her at all was Gaston, the portly, middle-aged butcher, who flirted with her whenever she stopped to pick up the day's order of *biftec* or lamb chops. And since he was married with five children, he hardly counted as a conquest.

"If you cannot compete, do not try," Giselle said as she slid the tray of croissants into the oven. "Your charm can be your novelty. Besides, the men here for the wedding are Americans. It may be they prefer an American woman."

She thought again of Marc and wondered what kind of woman he preferred. He'd been dismissive of his cousin's decision to marry, but men liked to joke about such things, didn't they?

She had no time to ponder the question further as guests began to fill the dining room. Lacey was preparing omelets while Giselle baked more croissants when an impeccably dressed white-haired woman entered the kitchen, the scent of

L'Air du Temps trailing in her wake. *"Bonjour, mes amies,"* she greeted them.

"Bonjour, Madame Beaulieu," they replied. Celeste Beaulieu was related somehow to the bride's family. It was she who had arranged for them all to stay at Milles Fleurs.

"Maybe I pour you some coffee, *madame?"* Lacey asked. "Giselle has some fresh made."

"No, no, no, don't go to any trouble," she waved away Lacey's offer. "I only stopped to see if you needed anything else from me for tonight's welcome dinner."

"Everything is taken care of," Giselle assured her. "You have only to enjoy the meal and your guests."

"And the pastry chef is arriving Friday to oversee the creation of the wedding cake. You are prepared to assist him, *non?"*

"Oui, madame. It will be my pleasure." Giselle's smile tightened a little with the words. Lacey knew she wasn't crazy about turning over her kitchen to another chef, but the family wanted this specialist, Monsieur Gautier, so Giselle had no choice but to relent.

"Wonderful." Madame Beaulieu clapped her hands together, clearly delighted. "Madame Ortolon tells me the inn is full. Everyone has arrived. We will have a beautiful week, and a beautiful wedding."

"All weddings are beautiful, are they not?" Giselle said, turning once more to her croissants.

"Yes, but a wedding in Paris, that is the most beautiful of all, I believe." *Madame* smiled at Lacey.

Lacey nodded and turned her attention once more to the eggs. Though the excitement of helping with the wedding preparations remained, she couldn't help but feel a little melancholy, too. As she had told Marc, being around lovers made one more aware of one's own loneliness. Her fantasies of the perfect man were entertaining, but she was ready to find the real thing. Paris was a city made to be enjoyed in the company of a lover.

DESPITE HIS EXHAUSTION, Marc spent a restless night. Uncle Frank's words rubbed at him like a rock beneath his mattress. *There are more important things in life than a job. People, and your relationships with them...*

It wasn't as if he didn't have friends. He got along well with the other photographers and writers with whom he often traveled. And he rarely went long without a woman in his life. He just wasn't ready to settle down. He didn't need all the closeness and romance most women wanted.

Still, he had to admit his life these days revolved around work. It might be that he could use a little more balance. He could start by taking his uncle's advice and trying to relax this week.

He finally fell into a deep sleep and woke late. Half-afraid he'd missed breakfast, he dressed hastily, grumbling as he maneuvered in the narrow space between his bed and the wall, and made his way downstairs.

The first person he spotted was the little American cook. She was exiting the kitchen with a large silver tray of still-steaming croissants. Marc rushed to hold the door for her. "Good morning," she greeted him in English. "You're looking much better today, Mr. Kendrick. Did you sleep well?"

"Eventually, yes." He followed her into the dining room, where she transferred the croissants to a laden buffet table. "I'm glad I ran into you," he said.

"Oh?" Her cheeks were very pink beneath a fall of dark hair. Was she flushed from the heat of the kitchen? Or from something he had said or done? The idea intrigued him.

"I didn't even get your name."

"It's Lacey. Lacey Jessup."

She turned back toward the kitchen and he held the door open for her once more. "You're American?" he asked.

She nodded. "I'm from Iowa. I'm in Paris studying at Le Cordon Bleu."

That explained the chef's uniform. "I wanted to apologize for my abruptness last night," he said. "My only excuse is that I really was exhausted."

"It's all right. You weren't that bad."

Her smile dazzled him. He might even have forgotten to breathe for a moment. It wasn't that she was extraordinarily beautiful. She was pretty in a wholesome way, but her chief attraction lay in the way she was so completely focused on him—as if there was no one else in the room.

"You're in a wonderful place to relax now," she said.

"I am?" An inn crowded with relatives and soon-to-be-relatives hardly seemed the ideal place to rest.

"Of course." She laughed. "Paris is one of the most beautiful cities in the world. The wedding isn't for five days, so you have plenty of time to explore. Unless—" she glanced at him out of the corner of her eye "—you've seen the city so many times before you're bored with it."

"The only part of Paris I've really seen is the airports." He'd passed through many times on his way to other parts of the world, but had never taken time to see anything outside the terminal. The thought of doing so now, alone, held no appeal. But with a pretty female for company… "Maybe you could show me some of the city, if you have time."

She stared openly at him, obviously surprised by the invitation. He cursed his impulsiveness. She probably had some hulking French boyfriend who liked nothing better than to pound hapless Americans. Or else she was still so put off by his rudeness last night she didn't want to spend one more minute in his company, much less a morning or afternoon. He tried for a graceful exit. "Of course, if you're busy…"

"No." Her expression relaxed, and she fixed him with a smile that once more momentarily stunned him. "Today I have class, and I have to help prepare tonight's dinner. But tomorrow I'm free all day after breakfast. I'd love to see the city with you."

"All right then. Good." He stepped back, detesting the sudden awkwardness that had him tripping over his own tongue. "I'll see you tomorrow after breakfast, then."

He whirled and exited before he made a bigger fool of himself.

Of course there was no such thing as solitude in which to brood in an inn full of wedding guests. He was filling his plate from the buffet table when Gabe's sister, Gina, stormed into the room, followed by her mother, Audrey. "I can't believe you forgot to pack your shoes," Audrey said, her voice rising above the low murmur of conversation in the room.

"Mom! It's just shoes," Gina said as she helped herself to coffee. "I'll just go today and buy another pair." She grinned. "Or three. After all, this *is* Paris."

"Those were dyed to match your dress." Audrey filled her own cup. She had the harried look of a woman with very many details to see to and not a great deal of time to devote to the matter.

"But they don't have to match, do they?" Gina

said. "I mean, it's not like everyone's going to be looking at my shoes."

"If your shoes don't match, then everyone else will have to change," her mother said.

Gina shrugged. "So?"

They drifted out of earshot. Marc grimaced at his plate. This was what he had to look forward to—five days of uproar over trivial matters like the color of shoes, the length of hems and place settings at the dinner table. It was enough to make any man want to become a monk.

Right now, though, he'd settle for breakfast in peace. He was searching for some place to sit when he was literally accosted by the erstwhile bride-groom, Gabe, and dragged by the elbow to a table in the corner. "Marc, I want you to meet my future wife, Alexis Donovan. Alex, this is my cousin Marc Kendrick."

At the words "future wife" Alexis, a stunning blonde, gazed at Gabe with an impossibly tender expression that made Marc want to retreat to the farthest reaches of the building. But of course he was stuck here, Gabe still gripping his arm. "It's nice to meet you, Alexis," he said. "I don't know how my ugly cousin here managed to persuade such a beautiful woman to date him more than twice, much less marry him."

Gabe's grip on Marc's arm tightened and Marc struggled not to wince; obviously, his cousin had been working out. "As you can tell, I got the biggest share of the family charm," Gabe said. "Marc's spent far too much time away from civilization, hanging out with terrorists and other unsavory characters."

Marc sent Gabe a look that let him know he would pay for that one, then assumed a kinder expression for Alexis's benefit. After Gabe's last statement, she was looking a little alarmed. "I'm a photojournalist," he said. "I photograph the bad guys, I don't 'hang out' with them."

"That sounds fascinating," Alexis said. "Would you like to join us for breakfast? I'd love to hear more about your work."

"Can't do that, honey." Gabe released Marc's arm and helped Alexis out of her chair. "We promised my mother we'd take her shopping this morning."

No doubt Gabe remembered the times his girl-friends had defected to Marc. Not that Marc had *tried* to steal Gabe's dates, but women seemed to prefer Marc's aloofness to Gabe's charm. He supposed they saw him as a challenge, though they usually ended up disappointed when they found they couldn't change him. No doubt agreeable men like Gabe were easier to love.

Gabe and Alexis said goodbye and Marc sat at the table they vacated.

Lacey entered the dining room again, this time with a fresh carafe of coffee. She went around the tables, refilling cups, until she came to Marc. "Giselle says her coffee is the sure cure for jet lag," she said, topping off his cup.

"Giselle—that's the Frenchwoman in the kitchen? The one who doesn't approve of me?"

He suspected she struggled against a smile. "Giselle doesn't approve of very many men," she said. "I wouldn't take her attitude personally."

"I seldom take things personally." He sipped from the cup and sighed. "She does make good coffee, though."

"I'll tell her you said so."

"Will that earn me brownie points with her?"

"Maybe. She might even slip you a larger serving of dessert at dinner tonight."

"You think I have a sweet tooth, then?"

"I wouldn't begin to speculate on your appetites, *monsieur*." With a saucy look, she turned and sauntered to the kitchen.

He laughed, his mood considerably lightened by the exchange. Lacey was a little too wholesomelooking to pull off the role of coy seductress, but he liked that she had a sense of humor. He couldn't remember the last time a woman had made him laugh, which made him feel considerably better about his decision to ask her to go sightseeing with him. Lacey might be the one thing that helped him get through this wedding with his sanity intact.

CHAPTER THREE

THE NEXT MORNING, Lacey rushed through the breakfast preparations, her mind fixed on the day ahead. Though she had explored Paris some on her own, walking the streets by herself wasn't the same as having someone to share the sights with. Paris was a city for couples—Audrey Hepburn and Cary Grant; Leslie Caron and Maurice Chevalier; Juliette Binoche and Johnny Depp.

Of course, Marc wasn't her lover—she didn't even know him that well. But he was a handsome young man and that was enough for an exploration of the city together.

"Your head is in the clouds this morning, *chérie*," Giselle chided as she took a basket of onions from Lacey's hand and replaced it with a basket of oranges for the buffet table. "What has you so distracted?"

"Oh…nothing," she lied, and darted toward the door to the dining room.

"I know what it is," Giselle said. "It is one of those handsome Americans, *non?*"

Lacey stopped and stared at her. "Why do you say that?"

Giselle smiled her cheshire-cat smile. "Because when a young woman is in a fog, the cause must be a man, of course." She waved a wooden spoon like a magic wand. "Not to mention you are wearing your very best skirt beneath your tunic. I am quite sure you did not dress up for me."

Lacey glanced down at the straight black skirt that just peeped from beneath the hem of her white tunic. When she removed the tunic and substituted beribboned ballet flats for her working clogs, she would be dressed in true Parisian style, simple but elegant, her red boat-necked sweater drawing attention to her neck and collarbone and—she hoped—away from a not-so-flat stomach, one of the hazards of always being in the kitchen and around food. "You're a very observant woman, Giselle," she said.

"*Oui*. Now off with you." She brandished the wooden spoon again. "The sooner you are done with breakfast, the sooner you may leave for your assignation."

Assignation. The word conjured up images of sultry kisses on the Pont-Neuf or lingering glances across a crowded bistro.

Reality was more mundane. Marc met her outside the dining room at nine-thirty. He wore tan slacks, a button-down shirt and a camel sweater.

But even in the more formal clothes he had the look of a man who spent a great deal of time outdoors. He had a camera bag slung over one shoulder. "I imagine you don't go anywhere without your camera," she said as he held the door for her.

"Old habit," he said. "Do you mind?"

"No. I think photography is very interesting. Where do you want to go?"

He shrugged. "What do you suggest?"

"It depends." She'd considered the question carefully all the day before. "They say one of the best ways to see the city is from one of the barge tours on the Seine. They pass by all the most famous landmarks."

He shook his head. "No barge tours."

She hid her disappointment. She had secretly longed to cruise the Seine on one of the tourist barges, leaning on the rail and taking in the sights, but again, it was the kind of thing that didn't seem right to do on one's own. However, if Marc wasn't interested... "If you like architecture, we could visit the grand cathedrals. Notre Dame, Sacre Coeur."

"No architecture. And no Eiffel Tower, either. Too many tourists."

She laughed at his snobbery. "But the whole idea today is to play tourist," she said. "I'm afraid we can't offer any wars or grisly scandals for your photojournalist's eye."

He frowned and she feared she'd offended him,

but he quickly relaxed. "Sorry. I just…I'd rather not stand in long lines to see the same sights everyone sees when they come to Paris. I can get that in a travel guide."

"Then what do you want to see?" she asked, at a loss.

He took her arm and guided her down the street, toward the Metro station. "Show me your favorite part of the city so far."

So that is how they ended up in Parc de la Villette.

"What is this place?" Marc asked as they stopped at the end of a long wooded promenade, the trees endlessly reflected in giant mirrors arranged on concrete pillars among them.

"It's the Garden of Mirrors," she said, leading the way down the walk.

"It's an outdoor fun house," he said, looking around them at their image and that of other visitors distorted by the many mirrors.

"Exactly." She laughed. "Now you know my secret."

"That you like mirrors?" He eyed her skeptically.

"That I'm drawn to the fantastic and absurd." From the Garden of Mirrors they passed a children's playground of turning windmills and flying sails and trampoline waves. "The Garden of Dunes," she said.

"There's something to be said for someone who appreciates the unusual," he said as they watched children bouncing on the air-filled "waves." "Is your whole family this way?"

She laughed again and shook her head. "No. They're all very solid, well-grounded citizens. I'm the only dreamer in the bunch."

He nodded. "So you came to Paris."

She glanced at him. His eyes met hers, warm interest in the gold-green depths. For a moment she forgot what she was going to say, mesmerized by that look.

"You came to Paris?" he prompted.

"Oh. Yes." She looked away, composing herself. "It's a good place for dreams, don't you think?" Dreams that would no doubt now include a certain hazel-eyed photographer.

"It has that kind of reputation," he said. He took her arm and they continued walking, into a terraced garden shaded by trellised vines. Dozens of fountains burbled musically among the vines and the scent of warm greenery perfumed the air. "What is this garden called?" he asked.

"The Trellised Garden." She leaned into him, enjoying the closeness. "What about you? Is your family full of artistic people like you?"

"No. My mother is a schoolteacher and I'm an only child." He paused by one of the small fountains. "I don't think I realized before now how many fountains and gardens Paris has."

"What about your father?" she asked.

His arm in hers went rigid. "What about him?"

She sensed she was entering delicate territory, but curiosity drove her onward. "What kind of work does he do?"

"Something in sales. I don't keep track. My parents divorced when I was ten." He moved away, distancing himself from her physically, the tension in his voice and on his face ending the emotional closeness they had felt as well.

"That must have been difficult," she said softly, following him from beneath the trellises.

"Yeah, well, I survived." They moved into an open area dotted with benches, flowers and kinetic sculptures.

"The Garden of Movement," she said, nodding to one of the abstract sculptures, which moved gently in the breeze.

"How did you find this place?" he asked.

"I got lost one day. I was trying to find a dress shop someone had told me about and I ended up here instead."

"Interesting place," he said. "Better than visiting a cathedral or the Eiffel Tower."

"Those places are nice, too, and you should see them while you're here. But this is different." She took his hand and pulled him down the walk. "I want to show you something." She led him to a glass dome suspended above the walk. "Stand here and wait," she said.

Then she hurried down the walk to a second dome. "Hello, Marc," she said.

"Hello," he said. "I can hear you perfectly."

"Yes." She laughed. "It's like the tin-can telephones we played with as children. Tell me a secret."

He was silent, then said, "No."

She suppressed her disappointment. "Then I'll tell you one." She thought of all the things she might say: *I'm very attracted to you.* Or *I sense a sadness in you that I want to understand,* but she couldn't find the courage yet to say these things out loud. So instead, she said, "Giselle uses frozen dough to make her famous croissants."

He laughed. "She'd probably fire you if she knew you said that."

"Yes, but I'm trusting you not to tell her."

They met again in the middle of the path. Marc was smiling, his earlier dark mood once more in retreat. "I've never met anyone like you," he said.

"I find that hard to believe. I'm very ordinary." She turned to watch a pair of elegant Parisian women stroll by. Everything about them spoke of style and culture, from their neatly coiled hair to their erect carriage and fashionable shoes.

"Maybe ordinary seems extraordinary to me because I've spent the last ten years chronicling the bizarre."

"You must have missed your family, being away

from them so much," she said. She had fought almost constant homesickness her first weeks in Paris.

"I can't say I missed them much." He glanced at her. "We've never been terribly close, though I've enjoyed being with them this week more than I'd anticipated."

She could not imagine being so cut off from her own family, or not having a real home for years at a time, as was the case with Marc. There was so much about him she did not understand, but still she was drawn to him.

He put his arm around her shoulders and they began walking again, across a small canal onto a black-and-white marble path that wound among the trees of a thickly wooded forest.

MARC COULDN'T SAY why he felt so at ease with Lacey. Maybe it was because he didn't feel the need to impress her or seduce her or do anything but relax. After all, he was only going to be in Paris a few more days, so there was no point in starting anything serious with her. Not to mention she wasn't his type. He preferred sophisticated, experienced women—ones who understood that not every relationship involved romance.

"This is the Garden of Islands," she said.

"It reminds me of part of Central Park," he said. There was the same sense of being in a wilderness in the midst of a bustling city.

"Do you live in New York?" she asked.

"I have an apartment there, though I'm not home much." Now that Nancy had moved out he expected he'd be there even less, at least for a while. While he never minded traveling alone, rattling around in an apartment by himself made him feel too…empty.

"Well, at least you've enjoyed seeing your family this week," she said.

"Yes… Some of them anyway. It's good to see Gabe, and Uncle Frank and some others. It's been a long time since we were all together like this."

"I don't have as big a family," she said. "But I do miss them." She sounded wistful. He imagined she had never traveled much before now and was probably homesick.

"You said you were from Iowa?" he asked.

"Yes. A little town called Ames. It's a nice place, though not very exciting."

"Not like Paris."

"No, not like Paris." She looked around as they exited the Garden of Islands and moved into a space where giant metallic kites hung in the trees overhead. "There's nothing like this in Ames."

He looked down at her upturned face, at the joy reflected there, and felt something give inside him—as if some binding had broken. He felt a little breathless and…lighter, if that was even possible. "I'd like to photograph you," he said.

A faint pink blush washed over her cheeks. "Me? Oh no, I really—"

"No. Please. Stay there, just as you were, looking up at the kites." He pulled his camera from the bag and snapped off the lens cover. Somewhat awkwardly, she stepped back and looked up at the kites again. But now she seemed stiff, the joy of the previous moment gone.

"Forget I'm here," he said. "Think about something that makes you happy. Something that makes you feel like flying with the kites."

As he spoke, she began to relax, her shoulders dropping, the stiffness going out of her smile. She looked up at the kites, then raised her arms at her sides, as if she would soar with them. He snapped off a series of shots, shooting from different angles. The joy in her expression was contagious and he couldn't help smiling.

"That was great," he said, letting the camera hang by the strap around the neck.

She laughed and rushed to his side. "I can't wait to see what they look like."

"Here, I'll show you now." He switched the camera to viewing mode and turned the screen toward her. One by one he scrolled through the images.

She covered her mouth with her hand. "Oh, my. I look a little silly, don't I?"

"Not at all. You look beautiful."

Their eyes met and held. Once more he had the dizzying sensation of free fall. His gaze shifted away, only to focus on her lips, so pink and inviting....

She stepped back, breaking the spell. Her face flushed, she fumbled with the clasp on her purse. "If you have the pictures printed, will you send me copies?" she asked.

"I will." They continued their walk. "What were you thinking about back there?" he asked. "When I was photographing you."

She smiled again, a secretive look. "I was thinking of the wedding, and how wonderful it would be to be married in Paris on a beautiful spring day like this one."

"And that made you so happy?" He would never understand this fascination women had with weddings and romance.

"Of course." Her smile broadened and he felt again the pull of her joy. "I was thinking of love. What could be better?"

What *could* be better? Especially if you were someone who had never known a love like that? A kind of love that seemed impossible to him, except when he looked at Lacey. Like the fantastic gardens she led him through, she made him believe all kinds of impossible things could become reality.

CHAPTER FOUR

WHILE THE WOMEN of the wedding party fussed and fretted about shoes, dresses, flowers and food, the men tried to stay out of the line of fire. They most often congregated at tables under the trees at the back of the inn's property, where they played poker and told stories, often involving outrageous adventures in their younger years.

Marc was surprised by how much he enjoyed those lazy hours spent with Gabe and his other cousins and Gabe's friends. After years of being on the go nonstop he'd expected to be bored by even a few days of forced family closeness. Instead, he found himself wishing the time would last longer.

The night after Marc's sightseeing trip with Lacey was the much anticipated bachelor party. The men descended en masse on Place Pigalle, to tour the city's red-light district. They began with dinner at Le Moulin Rouge, its famous neon red windmill revolving outside.

"Is it true the girls who dance the cancan don't wear any underwear?" Gabe's best man, Josh, asked.

"I don't know, but I guess we'll find out!" someone said.

But between the wine, the smoke and the dazzling lights, not to mention the swirling skirts and high kicks of the dancers, Marc couldn't say what the cancan dancers wore. Nor did he particularly care.

The men left the Moulin Rouge and joined the crowds on the street. Marc inhaled deeply, grateful for somewhat-fresh air after the smoky closeness of the cabaret. "Those French dancing girls are hot, aren't they?" someone said.

"They're pretty, but none of them look as good to me as Alexis," Gabe said.

This was greeted with groans, though Josh patted his friend on the back. "Spoken like a man in love."

Marc winced at the words, not because he didn't believe Gabe was in love, but because he'd only the moment before been thinking that none of the painted and exotically undressed women onstage looked as good to him as Lacey and her fresh-faced simplicity. But that certainly didn't mean he was in love with her. He scarcely knew her.

He shook his head, as if he could physically rid himself of such a ridiculous idea, and threw himself into the spirit of the evening. The men crowded into yet another cabaret and ordered over-priced champagne. Scantily dressed women descended on them and plied an embarrassed Gabe with kisses, until his face was covered in lip prints.

Marc lost track of the places they visited. One of the men had his wallet stolen by a pickpocket, while yet another drank too much and had to be bundled into a cab and sent back to the inn. Marc began alternating drinks with mineral water halfway through the evening, unwilling to risk his money or his life by losing his wits in the rough-looking crowd.

He did his best to enjoy himself, raising toasts to Gabe and tipping the dancing girls, but again and again he returned to the thought that he'd had a much better time the day before with Lacey.

At midnight, he found Gabe and told him he was headed back to the inn. "I'm packing it in," Marc said. "Guess I'm not the partyer I used to be."

"Don't go," Gabe said, his grin lopsided. "Don't leave me at the mercy of these animals." He indicated the others.

"You'll be fine," Marc said. "Just don't forget to come home to Alexis."

Gabe's expression grew dreamy. "Alexis. She's a wunnerful woman," he slurred.

"I'm sure she is." He patted his cousin's shoulder. "And she's lucky to be marrying you."

"You should get married," Gabe said. "There's nothing like knowing you're gonna be coming home ev'ry night to the woman you love."

"I'll leave that to you," Marc said. "I've never felt that way about anyone."

"Not yet. But I hope you do."

He left Gabe in the care of the other men and several dancing girls and went out onto the sidewalk and flagged down a cab. Gabe's last words echoed in his alcohol-fogged head. What *would* it be like to know there was always someone waiting for you? Always someone who loved you, who accepted your love in return? Lacey's face flashed into his head and he shut his eyes, dizzy. She was a woman he had just met. How could she be anyone special?

When he reached Milles Fleurs he was still feeling unsteady. He saw a light in the kitchen and decided to see if he could find some coffee. Caffeine and food would help clear his head.

The room was empty, though he was surprised to see bowls and cooking utensils had been left out on the counter. He smiled to himself as he searched the cabinets for coffee for the espresso maker in the corner. This must be another of Giselle's secrets—that she didn't always clean up the kitchen before she left for the day.

He had his head deep in a cupboard when he heard a startled cry behind him. He backed out of the cabinet and almost collided with Lacey, who cradled a bag of flour to her chest and gaped at him. "Marc!" She put a hand to her heart and laughed shakily. "You startled me. I thought you were a burglar."

"That's me. The coffee thief." He held up the bag of coffee beans he'd found. "I needed caffeine."

She smiled, and he felt a shakiness he couldn't entirely attribute to the alcohol he'd drunk. "Coffee sounds good," she said. "May I join you?"

"Sure. Do you know how to work that machine in the corner?"

"Let me do it." She took the bag of beans from him and gestured to the prep table. "You sit. How was the bachelor party?"

"Like all bachelor parties—a bunch of grown men trying desperately to hold on to the freedom of youth by drinking and ogling women." That was how he'd felt all evening—as if he was acting out an expected role, sampling the sinful wares of the red-light district because it was expected, not because it was anything he wanted.

"You make it sound terrible."

"Not that bad. Just not something I enjoy so much these days." He peered into one of the bowls on the counter and saw a lump of dough. "What are you making at this hour?"

"Brioche. It's for my basic pâtisserie class. The first batch came out horrible, so I had to start over."

She ground the coffee beans, then fed them into the machine, which began to purr like a cat. Soon the enticing odor of freshly brewed coffee filled the room.

"Why did you decide to go to the Cordon Bleu?" he asked.

"Because I like to cook. And because it was a way to see Paris."

"There are other ways to see Paris."

She nodded. "But I didn't just want to visit. I wanted to live here. To soak up the culture. The romance."

That word again. "Romance is important to you, isn't it?" He had never put much stock in romantic notions, thinking them the stuff of novels and movies. But watching Gabe tonight, hearing the tenderness in his voice when he spoke of Alex, Marc had been jealous. He had never known that kind of closeness to another person, and feared he never would.

"Romance is important," she said. "It's like… like the butter that gives the brioche its flavor. Without romance life would be as bland as bread without butter."

Had his life been bland? He refused to believe it, and focused instead on the rising dough in the bowl. "What did you do with the first batch?" he asked.

She stared at him for a moment, as if wanting to question the abrupt change of subject, then pressed her lips together and shook her head. "They're in here." She reached under the counter and produced a basket of misshapen rolls, some overbrowned. "I had the oven set too high." She laughed. "I still have trouble translating the French recipes, and adjusting centigrade and Fahrenheit."

He selected a roll from the basket and bit into it. "It still tastes good," he said. "Even better with butter and jam, I imagine."

She took the hint and produced butter and jam from the cooler, along with a thick crockery pitcher of cream for their coffee. When the espresso machine finished dripping, she poured two mugs of steaming café au lait. They sat across from each other at the counter, munching brioche and sipping coffee.

Marc found himself watching Lacey as she buttered a piece of bread and added a dollop of jam. Her hair was pulled back in a ponytail, but tendrils had escaped and curled around her face so that she resembled one of Lautrec's café-society women. She had a smudge of flour on one cheek and faint circles beneath her eyes, but he thought she was more beautiful than any perfectly made-up model or chic sophisticate.

"What are you looking at?" she asked.

He blinked, coming out of his daze. "What?"

"You were staring at me. Why?"

"You have a smudge of flour on your cheek."

She put a hand to her face. "Where?"

"Right…there." He leaned across the counter and reached up to wipe away the smudge. But when his fingers brushed her cheek, he stilled. Her skin was soft, as velvety as anything he could imagine. He wanted to savor the feel of her. To touch her more.

Their eyes met, hers dark and intense, filled not with fear or outrage at the liberties he was taking, but encouraging him to go further. She put her hand up to cover his and he moved closer, focused now on her lips. They were rose-pink, the lower slightly fuller than the upper, parted in a wordless invitation.

He bent and covered her mouth with his, his hand moving to the back of her neck to cup her head, cradling her as he parted her lips with his tongue and tasted her sweetness.

LACEY LEANED into him, eyes tightly shut, afraid if she opened them she might discover this was merely another of her fantasies. As soon as Marc had looked at her this evening, his hair tousled, his eyes slightly bloodshot, his expression that of a lost child, she had wanted to kiss him. To be kissed by him.

She gripped his shoulders and stood on tiptoe, leaning as close to him as she could get. If she'd been able to, she would have crawled right across the counter to press her body to his, to make love to him on the flour-dusted surface, the scent of coffee and strawberry jam mingling with their musk.

Instead, she had to settle for communicating her ardor with lips alone. He responded in kind.

With a groan, he deepened the kiss and threaded his fingers through her hair, freeing it from the elastic band so that it fell down her back. The muscles of his shoulders tightened beneath her hand. She kneaded them, the soft cotton of his shirt sliding against her skin.

A softly ringing bell startled them, and their lips parted, though they still held on to each other. "What was that?" Marc asked, his voice rough-edged.

"The…the timer." Reluctantly, she pulled from him and shut off the digital timer she'd set to remind her when to shape the rolls.

She avoided looking at him as she washed her hands. Now that she was no longer completely under the spell of his kiss, she wondered at the wisdom of abandoning herself to such passion. What good could come of losing her heart to a man who would only be in Paris a few more days? One who had chosen roaming the world and following adventure over the simpler things she loved?

"I'd better finish the brioche," she said, still not looking at him as she took the dough from the bowl and patted it into shape on the floured work surface.

"Yeah." He said nothing for a long moment; she could feel his gaze on her. "Thanks for the coffee," he said at last. "I'd better get to bed."

"Good night," she said, looking up in time to see him disappear through the door into the hallway. She sagged against the counter, a weariness that had little to do with the late hour dragging at her. Who was she kidding? It was too late to worry about losing her heart to Marc Kendrick. It was already lost.

CHAPTER FIVE

THE NEXT MORNING, Lacey looked for Marc at breakfast, but he wasn't there. Neither were the groom or most of the other male members of the wedding party. "They're all in bed nursing hangovers," Taylor, the bride's younger sister, said, rolling her eyes when Lacey commented on the men's absence. "Serves them right for staying out all night carousing."

"Wasn't the bachelorette party last night also?" Lacey asked.

Taylor grinned. "Yes, but I guess we women hold our liquor better."

Lacey returned to the kitchen and began mixing omelets. She doubted Marc was hungover. He hadn't seemed drunk at all when they'd talked in the kitchen last night. And she didn't like to think it was alcohol that had led him to kiss her.

It had been such a magical moment, that kiss. The stuff of dreams, but she was sure it was real. When she closed her eyes, she could almost feel his lips on hers again, his hand caressing the back of her neck.

"If you don't watch those eggs, they will burn," Giselle reprimanded her.

"I'm sorry." Lacey turned her attention once more to the omelet pan. "I was up late last night, working on my brioche."

"I saw." Giselle's expression softened. "It turned out perfectly, *chérie*. You are coming along."

"Thank you, Giselle. Coming from you that means a lot."

"Forgive me if I am a terror this morning," Giselle said. "The pastry chef comes tomorrow and I am not looking forward to sharing my kitchen. Especially with a man who no doubt thinks he is better than the rest of us who wear the toque."

"I'm sure you will charm him," Lacey said. "And no doubt you will be able to teach him a thing or two about baking. You've certainly taught me so much."

"You are a dear one." Giselle smiled. "Now hurry with the omelets. Then you can help carry coffee to the *invalides* upstairs."

She half hoped Marc's name would be on her room-service delivery list, but it was not. She took coffee to a grateful Gabe and Josh and two other cousins, then hesitated outside the door of Marc's bedroom/pantry before moving on.

An hour later she finished in the kitchen and went upstairs to change. She didn't have classes until that afternoon, and thought she might walk to the library. Anything to get out of the inn, where the possibility of seeing—or not seeing—Marc had her nerves on edge.

She was surprised to find a note, addressed to her in an unfamiliar hand, tacked to her door. She tore open the envelope and read it:

Lacey,
I thought I had better apologize for what happened last night in the kitchen. Blame my poor behavior on the late hour or too much to drink, or even the fact that I've been out of the country so long I've forgotten my manners. I feel as if I took advantage of your friendship and I'm sorry for that.

> Your friend,
> Marc

She stared at the words on the inn stationery until they blurred, then wadded the letter into a ball and fired it at the trash can by the desk. Then with a cry she retrieved the note and tried to smooth it out, finally tucking it between the pages of one of her schoolbooks.

How dare he apologize! As if she were a child who wasn't old enough to know what she wanted! How dare he try to pass off that wonderful kiss as a lapse of manners or the effect of too much alcohol. How dare he!

Before she lost her courage, she rushed from her bedroom, and down the stairs to Marc's room. She pounded on the door, not caring if his whole family heard her. "Open this door, Marc," she said. "I know you're in there."

The door opened so quickly she almost fell into his room. He caught her and pulled her inside. "What are you doing here?" he asked in a hoarse whisper.

"What's wrong with you?" she demanded. "Do you have laryngitis?"

"No. But I don't want anyone to hear us."

"Why? Are you ashamed of me? Is that why you sent that horrid note?"

"Horrid note?" He frowned. "If you mean my apology, what was so horrid about it?"

"Why did you think you had to apologize?" She stabbed a finger at his chest, backing him up against the bed. "I *wanted* you to kiss me last night. I wanted you to do more than kiss me and I think you wanted it, too. Why are you scared to admit it?"

"Scared?" He stood up straighter and captured her hand in his. "What do you mean, scared?"

"Practically from the first moment I met you, you've talked about how you don't believe in romance and sentimental nonsense and all of that. And yet many moments we've spent together have been some of the most romantic I've spent in my life. Why can't you see that?"

His hand around hers relaxed, and his other

hand caressed her shoulder. "Maybe because I haven't had much practice."

"Then you can practice with me. Right now that's what I want, more than anything." She stood on tiptoe to kiss him, a gentle brush of her lips against his that quickly turned more fevered as his arms went around her and he pressed his mouth more firmly against hers.

The kiss the night before had been like the bit of dark chocolate offered with fruit at the end of a meal—sweet and tantalizing. This morning's kiss was the full fudge torte, rich and decadent, tempting one to gluttony.

There was no work counter between them now, no brioche waiting to be baked or fear of interruptions to hold them back. Their focus was solely on each other—the feel of their bodies fitting so perfectly together, the soft brush of lips, the silken twining of tongues, the sensation of being so attuned to one another, of never wanting the moment to end.

They fell back on the bed together, hands exploring, learning the softness and hardness of each other's bodies even as their lips remained pressed together. She arched against him as he squeezed her breast, and reached around to fumble with the buttons of his shirt. It didn't matter that it was the middle of the morning, or that they were surrounded by an inn full of people who might hear their lovemaking. They were concerned only with each other, and the sensations building between them.

The knock on the door was as loud as a pistol shot, freezing them where they lay. It came again, followed by a man's hearty voice. "Marc, open up. It's me, Alan."

Marc's face went dead white and he gripped Lacey's arms so hard she was sure he left bruises. "Marc, what is it?" she asked. "You're hurting me."

He released her and sat up on the edge of the bed. "Shh, he'll hear you," he whispered.

"Come on, Marc, open up. I saw Frank downstairs and he told me you were here."

Marc continued to look ill. He buried his face in his hands. Lacey knelt beside him, anxious to comfort him. "Who is that?" she whispered.

He raised his eyes to meet her, sadness—and was that fear?—reflected back at her. "It's my dad," he said.

Marc listened as Alan continued to pound on the door. The man might not have been around when Marc needed him, but now that he was in the way, he wasn't about to give up.

"You'd better open the door," Lacey whispered. "Or the whole house is going to come to see what's the matter."

He nodded. "But he can't find you here."

No, it wouldn't do for a female staff member to be found in a male guest's bedroom.

She looked around the small room. "I don't see how we can avoid that."

"Hide under the bed. I'll get rid of him as quickly as I can."

She started to protest, then nodded. He helped her scoot under the bed, then pulled the coverlet over until it hung down to the floor. "All right, I'm coming!" he called. "Give me a chance to finish dressing."

He rebuttoned his shirt where Lacey had unfastened it, then raked a hand through his hair, took a deep breath and opened the door.

No matter how much Marc might have wished he could deny his paternity, all he had to do was look at Alan to know they were father and son. Alan Kendrick was a fleshier, grayer version of Marc. "What took you so long?" Alan asked, pushing past him into the room.

How many times had Marc wanted to ask his father the same question? "What are you doing here?" he asked.

"I was invited. Your mother and I may be divorced, but Gabe, at least, still considers me part of the family." Alan looked around the small room. "What is this, a broom closet? You should come to our hotel. Four stars and a great view of the Eiffel Tower."

"I prefer being here with the rest of the *family*."

Alan didn't even notice the slight. "So I hear

you're photographing the wedding. That's a bit out of your line of work, isn't it?"

Marc ground his teeth together. Why did everything his father say sound like a challenge? "I'm doing it as my wedding present to the couple. And as a favor to Uncle Frank."

"I hope they appreciate it. Margie showed me that piece you did in *Life* on Afghan refugees. Really good stuff."

The compliment caught him off guard. He knew manners required him to say thank-you, but he couldn't get the words out of his mouth. "Is Margie with you?" he asked instead. Margie was Alan's third—or was it fourth?—wife. She was a plump, pleasant person, older than most of his father's girlfriends.

"Yes. She said she'd always wanted to see Paris, so I thought, why not? You know how much women appreciate all that romantic claptrap."

No wonder Alan had been married three—or four—times, with an attitude like that. As soon as the thought crossed his mind, Marc thought of Lacey, and her accusation that he was afraid of romance. Well, who could blame him, with a father like this one? He'd learned from an expert how not to be close to people—or let them get too close to you.

"What do you want with me?" he asked.

"I want to see my son. To see how you're doing, find out what's going on in your life."

"It's a little late for that, don't you think?"

Alan frowned, looking older than his years. "That's old news, son. I'm sorry things worked out the way they did, but we have to move on from there."

"Then I guess you and I are headed in different directions." He rubbed his temple, where pain pounded like rhythmic blows from a hammer. "If you'll excuse me, I have some things I need to do."

Alan studied him for a long moment, then shook his head and turned to leave. "I'll see you around," he said.

"Yeah. See you around."

Marc closed the door after his father, then leaned his head against the hard wood, willing himself not to think. He'd cut ties with Alan years ago, so why did seeing the man always upset him so?

In the tension of the moment, he'd forgotten all about Lacey until she gently touched his shoulder. "Are you okay?" she asked.

He raised his head and looked into eyes so full of concern they made his throat tighten and ache. "I'm fine," he managed to croak. "Just…fighting a headache."

She nodded. "So that was your father."

"Yes." How many times over the years had he wished that wasn't the case?

"When was the last time you saw him?"

"He pops up every so often, tries to insinuate

himself back into my life." He turned away. "I don't really want to talk about him, okay?"

"All right." She sounded hurt, but he couldn't do anything about that. Alan Kendrick was a subject best left alone.

Lacey touched his back in a brief gesture of comfort, then pulled away. "I guess I'd better go," she said.

He nodded. "I'll see you later." Later, when he'd pulled himself together enough to face her. No telling where things would have ended up between them if Alan hadn't interrupted, but the mood was destroyed now.

"*Au revoir,*" she said softly, then closed the door behind her.

He sank to the bed and clutched a pillow to his chest, squeezing it hard, as if in doing so he could squeeze out the pain that welled inside him—old hurt and fears and regrets. The past was a weight around his ankles, making it difficult to stride into the future. Much as he tried, he'd yet to find a way to sever that burden.

CHAPTER SIX

LACEY SLIPPED out of Marc's room, her earlier elation overshadowed by sadness. The look in Marc's eyes when he'd realized his father was outside the door had made her heart ache. For a moment, she had glimpsed the boy inside the man—the boy who had been abandoned by the person he loved most. And in the conversation she'd overheard while under the bed, she'd sensed a man who still wanted his father's love but was too proud—or too afraid—to ask for it.

It had been all she could do not to crawl out from under the bed and demand that they both stop being such...such *men* and really listen to each other.

But relationships were not like recipes, she reminded herself. The same ingredients and actions were not guaranteed to produce the same results every time. And no one had asked this cook to get involved. The two men would have to work this out for themselves. Maybe being here in this wonderful place, with family for the happy occasion of a wedding, would help them settle their differences.

She was halfway to the stairs when a familiar voice called to her. "Mademoiselle Lacey. Wait a moment, *merci*."

She turned and waited for Celeste Beaulieu to join her. Today the matriarch was dressed in a pink suit that no doubt bore a designer label, her hair and makeup perfect as always. Lacey hoped *she* looked as good when she was old enough to be a great-aunt.

"I saw you coming from our handsome photographer's room." Madame Beaulieu leaned close and spoke in a conspiratorial tone. "The morning is a lovely time for an assignation, *non?*"

Lacey flushed. "I...I was just delivering room service."

"*Mais oui!* It is the room service every man should be so lucky to receive." Madame Beaulieu laughed. "Do not think I mean to scold, *chérie*. In truth, I am envious. When a woman reaches a certain age, such opportunities for romance are fewer, but I still remember the incredible feeling of not wanting to wait a minute longer to be with my lover."

"Marc and I aren't...that is, we..."

Madame Beaulieu laughed again. "If you are not yet lovers, I predict you will be soon. I have seen the way you look at one another."

"How is that?" Lacey asked, genuinely curious.

"With great heat and also tenderness." The older woman patted her hand. "Do not be embarrassed by this. You are young—do not be afraid to follow the desires of your heart."

She spoke with such certainty and wisdom, qualities Lacey felt she herself lacked, especially when it came to Marc. "But…I hardly know him," she said. "How do I know what I'm feeling is real?"

Madame Beaulieu's smile was as bright and warm as the golden Paris sun. "How do you know you are in love?"

Lacey nodded.

Madame Beaulieu tapped Lacey's chest. "Listen to what is in here. Love comes from the truest part of ourselves. If you listen to your heart, you will know. After all, why should it be so strange to love someone you have only just met? Our first impressions of people are usually the most accurate. When we first meet someone, we are forced to rely on our intuition instead of our logical minds. It is the same way with love, I think." She stepped back, a mischievous twinkle in her eyes. "After all, you are in Paris, in the spring, when anything is possible, *non?*"

Lacey nodded. Anything *did* seem possible in the City of Light. Even for as unlikely a pair as an Iowa farm girl and an acclaimed international photographer to be happy? The notion tempted her, but her mother's warnings to find someone more like herself and her own experiences with men who were all wrong for her held her back. If only she had a recipe for cooking up the perfect love affair—one that would turn out right every time.

MARC'S FEELINGS WERE as snarled as film ripped from a camera and left in a heap on the darkroom floor. He had forgotten everything else in those moments when he was kissing Lacey. In her arms, he'd been ready to believe anything was possible— even something as crazy as falling in love with a woman he'd known only four days.

Then his father had knocked on the door, recalling Marc to reality. In the real world, love led to loss. People were undependable. They left and you were powerless to keep them from walking away. It didn't matter if you were a little boy or a grown man, the pain was the same.

When he'd first picked up a camera, he'd found a way to lessen the pain. Observing life through a lens put him in control. He could frame the world the way he wanted and distance himself from the emotion of the moment.

So he turned to the camera again this morning. After all, he had a job to do. He'd promised Gabe and Alex some candid shots of the wedding party. Focusing on the people around him would help him forget his own troubles for a while.

On the way downstairs he met the older woman

everyone called Aunt Celeste. She smiled and startled him by winking as he passed, as if she was privy to an amusing secret about him. He shrugged. Maybe the old gal was flirting with him. She'd probably been a pistol in her day.

He took his camera into the garden. At this hour— or perhaps due to the aftereffects of last night's bachelor party—the area was quiet. He spotted movement over by the gazebo and walked quietly toward it, not wanting to disturb whoever was there.

Gabe and Alexis sat side by side on a bench just inside the gazebo, their heads together, talking quietly. Marc positioned himself behind a flowering shrub and focused his camera on the couple. They looked so serious. Was Alexis upset because Gabe had partied a little too hard last night? Was she angry enough to call off the wedding?

The thought made Marc's stomach hurt. Even though he didn't believe in happily-ever-after for himself, he wanted it for Gabe and Alexis. They seemed so perfect for each other, and they'd been so happy.

Gabe took Alexis's hand in his, and she raised her head and smiled at him. Relief surged through Marc and he clicked the camera shutter, capturing the love and intense happiness on the faces of the bride and groom. Then he slipped away, before his presence broke the spell they were under.

Finding no one else in the garden, he returned

to the inn, to the side parlor where guests often gathered to read or visit. He found the room unoccupied and turned to leave. But as he reached the door, it opened and Josh, Shannon and Taylor came in. "Marc!" Josh greeted him. "I've let these women talk me into playing Monopoly with them."

"I was in here yesterday and found a French version of the game," Taylor said. She opened an armoire and pulled out a battered cardboard box.

"Would you like to join us?" Shannon asked.

"No. But I'd like to stay and take some pictures. I promised Alex I'd get plenty of candid shots."

"I don't mind," Taylor said. She opened the box and began handing out playing pieces. "The car for you, Josh. Shannon, your favorite is the wheelbarrow, right? And I'll be the Scottie dog."

Marc moved to the other side of the room. As the other three began playing, he snapped off a series of shots, focusing particularly on the best man and maid of honor, who were seated on opposite sides of the card table. He smiled to himself, relieved at this reassurance that the house was not filled with lovers.

He raised the camera to his eye to frame a new shot, and froze. Though Josh and Shannon appeared to be focused on the game, indifferent to each other, he noticed how often they glanced at one another. They unconsciously leaned toward each other and Shannon repeatedly crossed and uncrossed her legs. When Josh's hand accidentally brushed hers as he reached for the dice, she jumped.

Marc clicked the shutter, almost unable to believe what he was seeing. But the camera did not lie. He had spent most of his adult life using his camera to gather evidence of the truth in war zones and disaster areas. Now it was showing him that even when it came to personal relationships, the true story was not always in words and actions but in the emotions communicated by the look in another's eyes or the expression on their faces. Whatever Josh and Shannon's outward behavior, they were very much aware of each other—very much in lust, if not in love.

Pondering this, Marc slipped out of the room. He was so accustomed to focusing his lens on other people, he didn't often stop to think about the impression he made on others. What did they see when they looked into his eyes? What did his father see? What did *Lacey* see?

He should go to her and apologize for the abrupt way they had parted this morning. He'd been upset with his father, but that was no reason to take his feelings out on her. He hurried to the kitchen and pushed open the door, but Lacey was not in sight.

Giselle stood on one side of the center worktable, a starched apron over her flowered dress, her chef's toque flopped over one ear. She gripped the edge of the table and glared at the man who stood across from her, a stocky fellow dressed all in white, from his starched pants and tunic to his tall toque, which rose a foot above his head, straight as a bishop's miter.

"It is impossible for you to use my kitchen this morning, Monsieur Gautier," Giselle said, her voice frosty. "I have an inn full of guests to cook for."

"But Mademoiselle Fortier, I must begin work on the fabulous *gâteau* I am to create for the wedding." Monsieur Gautier smiled, his attitude all French charm. "When you see the masterpiece I have planned, you will understand why it requires two full days to create."

Giselle sniffed. "I do not see why you cannot create this supposed work of art at your studio."

"Non, non, mademoiselle." Gautier came around the table and took one of Giselle's hands in his. "The cake is far too delicate to risk transport. It must be made at the site of the reception. That is what the family have hired me to do. I am sorry if you were not informed."

"I did not think you would be here until later today." Giselle jerked her hand from his. "Much later."

"Ah, the information must have been lost in the translation." Gautier regarded her out of the corner of his eye. "As a professional, you understand how it is, dealing with foreigners."

Giselle's frown was less severe. "At least you

admit I am a professional, even if I am not some fancy pastry chef with a Cordon Bleu pedigree."

"But of course!" Gautier seized her hand again. "The reputation of the kitchen at Les Milles Fleurs is impeccable. I have heard your *boeuf en croquette* is the kind of dish a man might wish to taste at least once before he died, or his life would not be complete."

Marc half expected the haughty Giselle to slap such outrageous flattery off the pastry chef's lips, but to his amazement, she actually smiled. "*Monsieur,* you are too kind," she said, her cheeks quite pink.

"Mademoiselle Fortier, I would be most honored if you would assist me with the creation of this wedding *gâteau.* Together I am sure we could make it a most memorable dessert, fitting the occasion."

Giselle took a step away from him, her face assuming a more solemn expression. "*Monsieur,* I have my own work to do. If you cannot afford an assistant, that is not my problem."

"Most assuredly, I do not mean to insult you." Gautier rushed to apologize. "I would never regard one such as yourself as a mere assistant. The word I should have used was partner. Co-creator."

Giselle looked unconvinced. "As I said, *monsieur,* I have my own work to do. No matter how much you flatter me, that does not change."

"Of course, *mademoiselle.* I am impertinent.

But the fact remains that you must cook and I must cook, and there is only one kitchen. How may we work out a compromise?"

Marc could see that Gautier had her now. What would she do?

"There are two ovens," she said at last. "And we will share the worktable. All I ask is that you not interfere with my work as much as possible."

"Merci, mademoiselle." Gautier made a courtly bow. "You are most gracious."

Marc continued watching them from the half-open door, curious to see how this would play out. If Giselle went after Monsieur Gautier with a rolling pin, he wanted to be around to photograph the scene. In the meantime, he snapped several pictures of them together.

Gautier lifted a large hamper onto the worktable and began unpacking an impressive array of bowls, whisks, measuring cups and pans. From another hamper he pulled flour, sugar and mysterious bottles and boxes of ingredients. Giselle turned her back to him and began pulling her own cooking tools from the cabinets, but she glanced continuously in the polished steel surface of the refrigerator, which reflected Gautier's actions.

"Mademoiselle, do you prefer cinnamon or cardamom as the predominant note in the spice cake?" Gautier asked as he lined up his bottles and boxes along the edge of the worktable.

"Cardamom, of course," she said. "It is much more sophisticated."

"Of course." He nodded and plucked one bottle from the row. "And perhaps a touch of clove?"

"A touch, yes." Giselle put down the frying pan she'd been holding and turned to him. "So you are making a spice cake for the wedding?"

"A spice cake with a filling of preserved fruit, with marzipan and cream icing."

"That is too rich," Giselle said. "A wedding cake should be light. It should melt on the tongue. On such a day one does not wish to be weighed down by heavy food."

"This cake will melt on the tongue," Gautier said. "And the cream makes it very light. A fantasy of a *gâteau*."

"How many eggs are you using?" Giselle asked.

"A dozen eggs."

She nodded approvingly. "And of course you separate them and beat the whites and yolks separately."

"That is not necessary with this recipe."

"How can it not be necessary? The cake will be like lead if you do not."

"*Mademoiselle,* I will show you. Now hand me that bowl, *s'il vous plaît....*"

They were still squabbling when Marc left, debating the proper whisk to use and the correct measurement of cardamom. He wondered how long it would be before Giselle realized she had been lured into the role of Gautier's assistant after all.

Then again, perhaps this was what she'd wanted all along—to be involved in a way that would save face. Or perhaps other emotions were at work— the ones that drew men and women together to communicate without words.

He returned to his room and sat on the edge of his bed, reviewing the photos he'd taken this morning on the camera's digital screen.

There was Giselle and Gautier, nose to nose, the air around them charged with energy. Josh and Shannon, intent on each other, making love with their eyes, even as their casual posture denied it. And finally, Gabe and Alexis, radiant with happiness and the promise of the future.

Everywhere he looked, Marc saw people in love. Once more he felt envious. He'd thought himself above such sentimental nonsense before, but now he felt vulnerable in a way he never had. He felt an emptiness inside but didn't begin to know how to fill it.

He wasn't one to believe much in fate, but he couldn't help wondering if his being here now— at this inn, for this wedding, with his family all around him—was some kind of opportunity for him to try to figure out where he'd gone wrong, and how he could make up for what had been missing from his life so far.

CHAPTER SEVEN

WHEN IN DOUBT, bake something. Lacey had pretty much lived by this motto since she was old enough to put slice-and-bake cookies in the oven. So it was just as well that her confusion over her feelings for Marc coincided with the final exam in her pastry class, in which she was to create an original dessert and present it to the class.

The day before the wedding, she found herself up to her elbows in flour and sugar and a pile of cherries in the kitchen of the inn. She had decided to prepare a fresh cherry tart with a cream filling in a hazelnut tart shell. Her fingers were stained from pitting the cherries and she still had a small mountain of hazelnuts to shell and grind.

To make matters worse, Giselle and the pastry chef hired to create the wedding cake, Hugh Gautier, took it upon themselves to "help" her with the project.

"Ma chère, you should add almond paste to the filling to complement the flavor of the cherries," Monsieur Gautier advised.

"Don't listen to him." Giselle elbowed Gautier out of the way. "Almond paste will make the filling too heavy." She gave Gautier a disdainful look. "The man does not know how to make a truly light dish."

"Perhaps because I have an appreciation of a dish with body." He eyed Giselle's behind and grinned wickedly.

Giselle squeaked and darted away, her cheeks bright pink, while Lacey choked back laughter.

"Incorrigible!" Giselle sputtered.

"*Mademoiselle,* it is true, you make me forget my manners." Gautier put his hands together in a pleading gesture. "Forgive me, but I find you irresistible."

"I am sure you say that to every woman in every kitchen in which you work," Giselle resumed her haughty attitude. "I know your type, *monsieur.*"

"You know nothing, *mademoiselle.* But if you will allow, we could know each other better."

Lacey added the hazelnuts to the food processor and switched it on, drowning out the bickering and banter. If Giselle had asked her advice, Lacey would have told her to respond to Gautier's flirtations. The older cook was obviously attracted to the dapper pastry chef, but pride or fear or some misguided belief about how she *should* act held her back.

Is that why Marc kept retreating every time the two of them got close? She added butter and sugar to the food processor and watched as the ingredients transformed into dough. She sensed he *wanted* to be with her, but his own history or his ideas about love, or *something* kept him from moving forward.

She emptied the dough into the tart pan she'd prepared and began shaping it into a crust. If only people would act on their feelings—follow their hearts, as Celeste had advised—and not *think* so much all the time. No doubt the world would be a better place.

She finished shaping the crust and began preparing the filling. "How are things coming, *chérie?*" Monsieur Gautier emerged from the pantry carrying the bottom layer of the wedding cake on a tray. Giselle followed with the next layer.

"It's going well, I think." She tasted the filling. It needed a little something. "I don't think almond paste is right for the filling," she said.

"What did I tell you?" Giselle looked at Gautier.

"But maybe—almond liqueur?" Lacey said.

"Amaretto. *C'est parfait!*"

"Not too much," Giselle cautioned. "You don't want to overwhelm the flavor of the hazelnuts and cherries."

"She is right," Gautier said. "Just a touch. A *soupçon.*"

"I have some amaretto here." Giselle turned to a cupboard.

"Allow me, *mademoiselle*." Gautier rushed to take the bottle down from the top shelf.

"*Merci, monsieur.*" Giselle looked almost coy and her face flushed once more, making her look much younger and less severe. Come to think of it, the two of them *had* been alone in that pantry for some time, Lacey mused. Perhaps they'd gotten better acquainted in more ways than one.

"Here you are, *mademoiselle*." Gautier handed her the bottle. "Try it now."

Under both older chefs' supervision, she added a small measure of the liqueur to her filling and whipped it in. They each tasted the results.

"Wonderful," Giselle declared. "If your instructors do not give you a top mark they are idiots."

"She is right again." Gautier beamed. "You have found just the right combination of ingredients, *chérie*. Congratulations. When you are graduated, perhaps you will come to work for me in my shop."

"Don't be ridiculous," Giselle said. "She is going to stay here and work for me." And the two were off once more, arguing all the way back to the pantry.

Lacey smiled and added the filling to her hazelnut crust. Her creation would be delicious—worth the effort it had taken to get it right. Maybe it was the same with relationships—the more effort one put into them, the sweeter the reward.

FOR THE WEDDING REHEARSAL DINNER, the dining room of the inn was transformed into a fantasy of tiny white lights and greenery. The ceiling and walls were draped in swaths of white netting, with strands of tiny lights glowing behind the fabric like starlight in fog. Potted palms were grouped around the room, while the table had been draped in white silk, and set with gold-rimmed china.

Marc, camera in hand, took his designated place at the table and found he was across from his father and Margie. The two men hadn't seen each other since the confrontation in his bedroom, but Marc had vowed to be civil. Alan had apparently taken the same vow. He nodded to Marc and said hello. "You remember Margie, of course," he said.

"Of course. Hello, Margie." Marc shook hands with his father's wife—he refused to think of her as his stepmother—and took his seat. The rest of the family joined them and the hum of conversation filled the room.

"It is so wonderful to have everyone together like this to celebrate this wonderful occasion." Celeste addressed them from her place at the head of the table. "I feel that love is in the air here. May we all fall under its spell." She raised her glass and they all toasted, then servers brought in the first course, a cream-based pumpkin soup that had everyone raving.

Marc looked up and caught his father watching

him. "You look good," Alan said. "All this traveling must agree with you."

Only a few days before, Uncle Frank had told him he looked worn-out. Had Paris made the difference, or something else? "I guess. I enjoy my work." He did enjoy the work, but the only real reason he tolerated the travel anymore was that he had nothing to come home to but an empty apartment. It was easier to stay busy and on the road than to face the loneliness of his life away from work—something this time spent observing all the couples around him made him feel more acutely than ever.

Uncle Frank stood and cleared his throat. Everyone turned their attention to him. "As the official host of this dinner, I want to welcome you all and say what a pleasure it's been getting to know you these past few days."

Applause and calls of "Hear, hear!" greeted this sentiment.

"I just want to say how happy we are to have Alexis and her family as part of our family," Frank continued. "She's a lovely young woman and I know she's made my Gabe very happy."

Gabe leaned over and stole a quick kiss from his bride-to-be. Marc joined in the applause. Gabe *did* look happy, but how long would the feeling last past the wedding? Was there really such a thing as happily-ever-after?

Throughout the main dish and the salad, Marc

studied his fellow diners and fell into a deeper and deeper funk. So much for joining in the celebration. Everywhere he looked he saw people who were happier than he was. Even his father and Margie were smiling and seemed truly enamored of each other.

He told himself he needed to snap out of his dark mood, but didn't know how.

The main course was followed by salad, then cheese. "We have a special treat tonight," Celeste announced when the cheese plate was cleared. "For dessert, we have a new dish, created by our own Mademoiselle Lacey Jessup."

On cue, the door to the dining room opened and Lacey appeared, bearing a silver tray on which rested several gleaming cherry tarts. "The cherry and hazelnut tart is Lacey's project for her pastry class at Le Cordon Bleu," Celeste explained. "It is so delicious, we are sure she will receive the highest mark. We are privileged to have her share her creation with us."

Lacey blushed a deep pink as everyone applauded, but Marc had never seen her smile so much. She was so beautiful it hurt him to look at her. She glanced around the table, stopping when she came to him, her smile warmer still.

His heart jumped in his chest, the sensation startling him. He had always suspected such physical reactions to another's presence were the fiction of novels. Yet his behavior when near Lacey never failed to catch him off guard. And likewise, he could never predict how she would behave around him.

He remembered her anger at his apology for kissing her the other night in the kitchen, and the memory made him smile.

"What's so amusing?"

Alan's question brought Marc out of his reverie. He shook his head and focused his attention of the slice of tart the server had set in front of him. "Just remembering something that happened," he said.

"Share the joke with me," Alan said. "These dinners bore me out of my skull." He took a large bite of tart and spoke around it. "The food's good, though."

Of course Alan was too self-absorbed to be interested in any activity that didn't revolve around himself. On another occasion, Marc would have pointed this out, but tonight he was reluctant to risk losing the pleasant feeling seeing Lacey had given him.

When dinner had at last ended, he went in search of Lacey. He found her alone in the kitchen, scrubbing down the worktable. "The tart was delicious," he said.

"Thank you." She didn't look at him but kept scrubbing, the muscles of her bare arms tensing with each stroke. "I was flattered when Giselle asked me to cook it for the dinner tonight." She laughed. "Though I suspect that may have had something to do with her determination not to give Monsieur Gautier the chance to contribute one of his own creations."

"Monsieur Gautier is the pastry chef?" he asked, remembering the man who had sparred with Giselle the day before.

"Yes, that's him. Giselle resents having to share her kitchen with him, plus she thinks he's too haughty and grand. But at the same time, she's very attracted to him."

"Hmm." He really didn't care about the pastry chef or Giselle; he only wanted to keep Lacey talking. He moved closer, to the edge of the work counter. The overhead lamp shone like a spotlight on her, bringing out red-gold highlights in her dark hair. He raised his camera to his eye and studied her through the lens, framing the shot.

"You're not going to take a picture of me like this!" she protested, stepping back.

"Go back to what you were doing," he said. "You look beautiful."

Her expression softened and her lips parted, as if she was about to say something, then she shook her head and returned to scrubbing the table with new vigor. He snapped off shot after shot, focusing on the soft curve of her shoulders, the paleness of her cheek and throat against the fall of dark hair, the long, slender fingers of her hands.

"Are you done yet?" she asked, straightening. "Because the table is clean."

He lowered the camera. Usually, he felt more vulnerable without the protection of the lens between him and his subjects, but with Lacey things were different. With her, everything was different. "Are you almost through here?" he asked.

She folded the dishrag over the sink and untied her apron. "I'm done."

"Will you take a walk with me?"

She turned to him. "Where do you want to walk?"

"It doesn't matter. This is Paris. It's supposed to be beautiful at night." *Especially if seen with the right person.* But he couldn't say that. Not yet.

"All right." She hung the apron on a hook by the door. "I'd like that." She let him lead her to the door. "You surprise me, though," she said.

"How is that?" He held the door for her, then followed after her.

"Because." She grasped his hand once more. "You told me the first night we met that you didn't believe in romance. Yet I can't think of anything more romantic than strolling hand in hand through Paris at night. Maybe there's hope for you yet."

"Maybe there is." They momentarily moved out of the glow of streetlamps and he was glad of the darkness to hide his expression. He could walk forever like this, holding her hand and saying nothing, enjoying the contentment of being in her presence. But she wouldn't be satisfied with that, he knew. Women wanted words, and somehow, tonight, he was determined to find the right ones to say to her.

CHAPTER EIGHT

PARIS AFTER DARK was a spectacle of sight and sound—the blare of a taxicab's horn, the Arc de Triomphe bathed in golden light, the accordion blare of street musicians, the lights on the bridges over the Seine like strands of pearls suspended over the water, the musical peal of laughter and rapid conversation. And over all the Eiffel Tower shone like a confection of gold spun sugar.

Lacey reveled in all of this as she and Marc walked along the Seine, but he seemed not to notice any of it, walking with his head down, his gaze fixed on the sidewalk.

She tucked her hand in the crook of his arm. "Is something bothering you?" she asked.

He lifted his head and stared into her eyes as if searching for some answer there. "You asked me about my father the other day," he said.

She nodded, waiting for him to continue.

He shoved both hands into his pockets. "I guess you figured out he and I don't get along."

"You said he and your mother are divorced."

"He walked out when I was ten. My mom came home from picking me up from school and there was a note on the table with a hundred-dollar bill, saying he was sorry, but things just weren't working out."

Lacey tried to imagine the shock and pain of such a thing, especially to a child. "How awful for you."

"Yeah, well, the next day my mom found out that hundred bucks was the only thing we were going to get. He'd cleaned out the bank account and left us literally with nothing." He glanced at her. "My mom got a job working in the school cafeteria during the day and cleaned houses at night to pay the bills."

"So your dad left and your mom wasn't around because she was working all the time," Lacey said.

"That's about the size of it." He blew out a breath. "When I was eight, my old man was my hero. He was always laughing and joking. Everybody liked him and I wanted to be just like him."

"I think most little boys are like that."

A tourist boat passed them, laughter and snips of conversation in French, English, German and other languages Lacey couldn't identify drifting over them. Marc turned his head to watch the boat pass. When it was gone, he said, "I spent the first year he was gone wishing he would come back. I used to dream about it. He'd walk in the door and we'd find out he'd been on some top-secret mission to save the world, or he'd been working around the clock in a secret laboratory, discovering a cure for cancer."

She smiled, picturing the little boy who'd dreamed such big dreams, and delighted to know his imagination had been as wild as her own. "Did you hear from him at all?" she asked.

He shook his head. "Not for four years. By then I'd grown to hate him. I blamed him for everything that was wrong in my life."

She tightened her grip on his arm. "Why did he stay away so long?" she asked.

"He said life got in the way—that I'd understand when I got older." He shook his head. "All I ever understood was that I couldn't depend on him for anything. And I didn't want to."

"You never forgave him," she said, stating the obvious.

"I never did. I don't know that I can."

They turned to admire the lit facade of Notre Dame, its wedding-cake structure looking surprisingly delicate at night, the dirt of centuries erased by shadow. Lacey traced the outline of buttresses and gargoyles and thought of how much the past can stay with a person. "So here he is again and you're stuck in the same place," she said after a moment.

"That's it exactly." Marc faced her. "So what do I do now? I'm thirty-two years old and I'm stuck feeling like a ten-year-old again. How can I make him understand I just want him to leave me alone?"

She hesitated, reluctant to offer advice he might not welcome. But the pain in his voice moved her to want to help him. "Maybe the problem isn't that he keeps pushing his way back into your life, but that part of you needs him there—and you can't find a way to bridge the gap between you."

He looked away and her breath caught in her throat.

"I've done fine without him all these years," he said. "Why would I need anything from him now?"

"I don't know." She put a hand on his shoulder, wanting to comfort him but powerless to do so. "But maybe you should ask yourself—are you punishing him, or are you punishing yourself?"

His eyes met hers again, hollowed shadows in the streetlight's glow. "What should I do?"

She laid her palm against his chest. His heart beat strongly, in rhythm with her own pulse. "A wise woman once told me to trust the desires of my heart. That will tell you the right thing to do."

WHEN LACEY TOUCHED HIM, Marc stilled, scarcely daring to breathe. Her face was turned up to the light, more lovely than any of the spotlighted monuments they'd passed. The faith in her eyes— faith in him—made him feel both invincible and more vulnerable than he'd ever been. *She* was the desire of his heart—at least in this moment.

He reached up and covered her hand with his own. "Do you think it's possible to feel a deep connection to someone you've only known a few days?" he asked.

Her eyes locked to his, she nodded. "I do."

He pulled her close and kissed her, pulling her tightly against him, his mouth firm against hers. The world around them shrank to the narrow space occupied by their bodies pressed together, the only sound their ragged breathing and pounding hearts, the only sensations the slide of warm flesh against cotton clothing, the taste of salty-sweet kisses, the faint floral scent of her perfume in the warm night air.

"Stay with me tonight," he murmured, his lips against her hair above her ear.

"Yes," she said. She drew back and looked him in the eye, her arms wrapped around his waist. "Yes, I'll stay with you."

He drew her head to his chest. She would be with him tonight. He wouldn't think any farther than that right now. No more mourning the past or worrying about the future, at least for this one night.

They returned to Milles Fleurs and slipped through a side door and up the stairs to Marc's room. Marc held Lacey's hand and led the way as they hurried on tiptoe, stepping carefully to avoid the one step that always squeaked, navigating by memory around obstacles in the dark hallway. Lacey's body hummed as if she'd drunk an entire bottle of champagne, giddy with the tantalizing air of secrecy and the anticipation of discovery.

Behind the locked door of Marc's room, they fell on the bed in an embrace, already fumbling with each other's clothes. Marc's fingers were clumsy on the buttons of her blouse and she reached up to help him. Only then did she realize he was nervous. The thought that this man of the world, who had traveled everywhere and photographed every kind of dangerous situation, should be unnerved by the idea of making love to her, touched her. She wrapped her fingers around his and gave him a long, slow, kiss. "We don't have to be in a hurry," she whispered.

"I don't want to risk us being interrupted again," he said.

She smiled. "If anyone knocks on the door, we won't answer."

"Sounds like a plan." He attacked her buttons again, with more assuredness this time, and soon she was free of her blouse and was wiggling her way out of her skirt. He stood and stripped out of his own clothes and they faced each other, clad only in their undergarments, lit only by a thin strip of moonlight that shone through the closed curtains.

"I'd love to photograph you like this," he said,

smoothing his hand down her arm. "In the moon-light, your skin like ivory."

"There's no need for photographs, when you have the real thing right here." She reached up and drew his head to hers, kissing him open-mouthed, tongues entwined. He cupped her breasts through her bra, then slid the straps from her shoulders and pushed aside the satin and lace to reveal her fully.

She gasped at the brush of his fingers across the soft underside of her breasts, and felt a dizzying rush of heat as he bent to take her in his mouth.

She reached back and popped the clasp on the bra and tossed it aside as they sat, then lay across the narrow bed. "I've been dreaming about this," he said, raising his head to look at her once more.

She smiled. "Those must have been interest-ing dreams."

"Yes. But nothing compared to reality." He slid one finger beneath the elastic of her underwear, moving it back and forth, teasing her. She smoothed her hands along his sides, feeling the ridge of each rib, fighting the urgency that made her want to demand that he take her quickly—now!

He nudged the panties down her hips, over her thighs, toward her ankles. She kicked out of them and he cupped her bottom in his palm. For one panicked moment she thought of cellulite and

sagging and all the weight she'd meant to lose but
hadn't, then he said, "You're beautiful," and the
reverent tone in his voice made her believe it.

Tonight, at least, she was beautiful—the most
beautiful woman in the world, as long as she lay
in his arms. She slid her hands up his shoulders,
everything in her that was feminine responding to
his strength and masculinity. She clasped her
hands behind his neck and arched against him,
feeling his erection hard against her belly, evidence
of how much he wanted her.

He rolled to one side and shed his own underwear,
then pulled her to him once more. They lay face-to-
face, staring into each other's eyes, their features
blurred in the dim light, every other sense height-
ened. When Lacey breathed in, the fresh-linen scent
of lavender and starch mingled with the musk of sex
in a heady perfume that aroused her even more.

"You smell like almonds," he said, kissing her
fingers.

"Amaretto," she said. "I spilled some when I
was baking. The scent lingers."

"I'll think of you every time I smell it now."

She started to make a joke about marketing her
cherry tart as an aphrodisiac, but he slid her finger
into his mouth, silencing her. A tightness, low in
her womb, grew with the pressure of his mouth,
until she was writhing beneath him.

"I don't...want to wait...any longer," she gasped.

He freed her fingers and propped himself on one elbow to look down at her. "Do you want to use a condom?" he asked.

She nodded. "Yes."

He rolled away from her and leaned down to reach under the bed. She heard him slide his suitcase from beneath them, and the rasp of a zipper, then he was beside her once more, ripping the condom packet with his teeth.

"Would you like to do the honors?" he asked.

She rolled the condom carefully over him, the sensation of heat and hardness in her hand making her clench her thighs together.

Then he was gently pushing her thighs apart and kneeling over her. She reached for him, inviting him in, welcoming him.

He moved slowly at first, filling her completely with a sigh of satisfaction that mirrored her own feelings. When he began to withdraw, she arched to him, matching his rhythm of advance and retreat, a deft partner in a dance that left her breathless and always wanting more.

She smoothed his hair, and murmured endearments even she could not make out. He cupped her bottom, bringing her more firmly in contact with him, and with his free hand began to stroke her breast. Every nerve in her was aware of the connection between them—both the physical sensations everywhere they touched, and the emotional bond that led them to move in concert, and to anticipate each other's needs.

When her climax came, she cried out, then, laughing, brought her hand up to muffle her shouts. Tears stung her eyes, tears of release and a joy she couldn't begin to describe. Marc's own release shook them both anew and afterward they remained entwined, rocking together, not speaking. Lacey feared words might break the spell that held them in thrall. If she gave voice to all she was feeling right now, would it frighten Marc away? He was a man who didn't believe in romance. Did that mean he didn't believe in love as well? Or was it only that he didn't know how to express that most mysterious of all emotions?

As she cradled his head on her breast, she closed her eyes and breathed a silent prayer that, somehow, Marc would see that love and romance were real. After all, what better place and time to learn, than in Paris, the city of lovers, a celebration of love itself.

NEARBY CHURCH BELLS were striking three when Lacey reluctantly disentangled herself from Marc's embrace. "I'd better go," she whispered. "We both have busy days today." The rough stubble of his beard grazed her cheek as she leaned in once more to kiss him—quickly, before she gave in to temptation and slid under the covers with him once more. These few hours in this little room, secluded by darkness and the late hour from all those sleeping around them had been the stuff of fantasy—the fairy-tale romance she'd often daydreamed about.

"Photographing a wedding party is a lot different from my usual work." Marc sat on the side of the bed and pulled on his jeans. "I'm used to action photos, pictures that tell a story."

"Your photos for the wedding will tell a story, too." She climbed over him and stood in the narrow space between the bed and the door, buttoning her blouse. "The story of two people in love, and all those around them that are celebrating with them."

"I guess so. But it's still different."

"I'd better go." She picked up her shoes but did not put them on. It would be easier to slip barefoot through the hall to her room. She stood on tiptoe and kissed his cheek, then let herself out of the room. *"Au revoir,"* she whispered. Until we meet again.

In the hallway, she let her shoulders sag, no longer intent on hiding her feelings from him. Their night together had been wonderful, but his last words had reminded her that he lived in a world so different from hers. Marc's was a world of excitement, adventure and danger, while Lacey surrounded herself with beauty, food and family. Even though she had chosen to move thousands of miles away from her home, family was still important to her. This week spent preparing for the wedding had reminded her of that. Marc was a man estranged from his family; she wasn't even sure he wanted to change that.

Her thoughts in too much turmoil to allow her to sleep, she went downstairs instead of up, intending to make herself a cup of chocolate before bed. She navigated the old wooden risers by feel, probing with her foot for each step, one hand grasping the balustrade.

So intent was she on the task that in the darkness she didn't see the figure approaching, until they collided at the bottom of the stairs. Lacey stifled a scream and a woman's voice responded with a string of muffled French curses.

CHAPTER NINE

"GISELLE, IS THAT YOU?" Lacey asked, startled to find her boss roaming the halls at this time of morning.

"Lacey?" Giselle reached over and snapped on a lamp that sat on a table at the foot of the stairs, and the two women stared at each other. "What are you doing up at this hour?"

Lacey tried not to stare at the older woman but couldn't help herself. Instead of her usual apron or tunic, Giselle wore a fashionable minidress and tights. Her hair was swept up in a chignon and her eyes were heavily made-up. She wore red lipstick, much of which was smudged. She carried a pair of chic heels in one hand. "I...I was going to the kitchen to make a cup of chocolate," Lacey said.

"Carrying your shoes?" Giselle nodded to the flats that dangled from the fingers of Lacey's right hand.

"I could ask you the same thing," Lacey said.

Giselle's face reddened. "I didn't want to wake anyone, coming in so late."

"Same here," Lacey said.

"But you were coming down the stairs…" Giselle's gaze drifted up, then she grinned knowingly. "I see. You are coming from an assignation with someone in this house."

"What about you?" Lacey asked. "You've obviously been out with someone." Her gaze fixed on the smeared lipstick and she hazarded a guess. "Was it Monsieur Gautier?"

"The man is impossible," Giselle protested. "He presumes to tell me how to cook and he thinks he is so charming."

"He *is* charming," Lacey said. "And even if you won't admit it, I think he's charmed you."

Giselle's smile was warmer now. "There is something to be said for a charming man," she said. "Come, let us go to the kitchen and make that chocolate. I also know where there are some decadent butter cookies I have been saving for a special occasion."

Once in the familiar sanctuary of the kitchen, Giselle tied on her apron and heated milk while Lacey grated chocolate. Giselle whipped the chocolate shavings into the hot milk until it frothed, then poured the drink into two thick mugs, topped with more shaved chocolate. She produced the tray of cookies and the two women sat on either side of the worktable.

"Ahh," Giselle said after her first sip. "Even the

great Hugh Gautier has not had chocolate better than this."

"I bet Monsieur Gautier likes you precisely because you're not impressed with him," Lacey said. "In any case, you've obviously enchanted him."

Giselle nodded. "When I am with him, I fall under his spell, but when we are apart…" She gave a Gallic shrug. "I wonder what I see in him. Or any man. They are all so full of themselves."

Lacey thought of Marc. She wouldn't have described him as self-absorbed. Rather, weren't all people, including her, caught up in their own lives? Learning how to mesh your life with that of another was one of the tricks of a successful relationship, she thought.

"And you, were you with that arrogant American, Monsieur Kendrick?" Giselle asked.

"Marc isn't arrogant," she said. "He's really very nice."

"They all are when they want you in their beds." Giselle sipped her chocolate. "Then again, a man's bed is not always a bad place to be. It's usually out of it that trouble starts."

"I think I'm in love with him."

Lacey hadn't meant to say the words out loud, least of all to Giselle, but there they were, hanging in the air between them.

To her surprise, Giselle did not mock or laugh.

"If it is true, I am happy for you," she said softly. "I only hope he returns the feelings."

"I don't know," she said. "I hope so, but…how do you know if love is enough?"

Giselle shook her head. "I am not the person to ask about love. I have not been lucky in love. But wasn't there a song…love is all you need?"

"But is it?" Lacey set aside her half-empty cup. "Marc and I are so different. He makes his living traveling to dangerous, exciting areas all over the world."

"Even world travelers like someone to come home to." Giselle studied her over the edge of the cup. "Besides, you are not exactly a homebody. You came all the way to France to study at Le Cordon Bleu. You could travel with him. Or he could decide to stay home with you. Or you could arrange passionate meetings all over the world in between assignments."

"That sounds like a strange way to live," Lacey said. "It seems to me the whole point of being in love is wanting to be together."

Giselle waved her hand. "People live all kinds of lives. Who says you can't have a great love if you don't see your lover every day?" She smiled. "Maybe it's even better that way. The passion does not fade from boredom."

Giselle made it all sound terribly romantic, but Lacey had her doubts. She enjoyed her daydreams, but she knew reality was not as neat and pretty.

"I've made mistakes before," she said. "Falling for the wrong man. My mother says I choose men who are too different from me—that if I want to be happy, I should find someone more like myself."

"Someone from Iowa, U.S.A., who also cooks?" Giselle arched her brow. "I think your mother was trying, the way mothers do, to keep you from leaving home." She chuckled. "She was probably afraid you would be swept off your feet by some charming Frenchman."

"Like Hugh Gautier?"

"Like Monsieur Gautier." Giselle stood and gathered their cups. "I will tell you what I tell myself all the time—men are not worth losing sleep over. Women spend too much time trying to contort themselves to fit the desires of the man of the moment. It is time we expected them to compromise for us."

"So I should ask Marc to live a different kind of life?" She shook her head. "I could never do that."

"You don't have to do that. But don't think you have to live a different life, either," Giselle said. "There are all sorts of ways of being in love. If this man truly returns your feelings, you will both find a way to make this work. If not—" she shrugged again "—then he is not worth having."

Later, Lacey lay in bed for a long while, Giselle's advice replaying over and over in her head. Marc was definitely "worth having." He was a man who made her feel things she'd never known with anyone—passion and tenderness, and her own ability to accomplish anything.

She believed Marc loved her, but was that enough—especially for a man who didn't believe in romance, a man who cut himself off from love and family because being alone was easier than risking being hurt? Lacey could promise Marc she would never hurt him, but such a promise would be a lie. Even she, with all her fantasies, knew that love sometimes hurt.

Marc risked everything to get the photographs that had made him famous. But how could she, a small-town girl whose one talent was cooking, convince him she was worth risking his heart?

THE DAY OF THE WEDDING DAWNED with the bright, clear light that had illuminated the work of famous Parisian artists for centuries. The wedding itself would be a work of art as well, from the masterpiece of a wedding cake that Monsieur Gautier and Giselle had worked late into the night assembling, to the flowers that filled the rooms of the inn that would today truly live up to its name of Milles Fleurs. The bride and her attendants were visions in silk and lace, made even more beautiful by the glow of love surrounding them.

Marc photographed the women in an upstairs bedroom of the inn as they primped and prepared for the upcoming ceremony. He shot Alexis with her attendants, and with her mother and her Great-Aunt Celeste. To his surprise, he found he enjoyed the work, joking with the women and positioning them for the best light. There was none of the urgency here he often felt on a photo shoot. The adrenaline rush that accompanied most of his work was replaced by a sense of accomplishment and ease.

As he wandered from room to room in the inn, and heard the warm greetings from everyone there, he was reminded that he was with family—the people who loved and accepted him not for what he'd accomplished in his life, but simply for who he was. Why had he avoided this feeling for so many years?

For the first time since his arrival at the inn he was able to look upon these wedding photos not as an obligation to be endured, but as his gift to the happy couple. The thought inspired him to work even harder to get the best shots possible, and the ones that would be most meaningful when they looked back upon this record of the day.

He took pictures of Gabe, who was pacing the hallway that led to the garden where the ceremony was to take place. "Times like these, I wish I'd taken up smoking," Gabe said, straightening his cummerbund for the twentieth time. "It would give me something to do with my hands."

"Alexis would never kiss you again," Josh said.

Marc photographed Gabe and the groomsmen together, then Gabe and Uncle Frank embracing. As he watched his cousin and uncle through the camera's viewfinder, Marc swallowed past a knot in his throat.

He had always told himself he would never enjoy a similar moment of closeness with his father, but last night's conversation with Lacey made him wonder if he did indeed have the power to alter that picture of the future.

He hadn't seen Lacey since she'd slipped from his room in the early hours of the morning. He'd stood in the doorway of his room and watched her tiptoe away, her bare feet soundless on the hall runner, nearby church bells pealing half-past three.

She was busy now, helping in the kitchen with preparations for the wedding feast. Later, he would find her and they would talk. They had so many things to discuss.

At the appropriate hour everyone gathered in the garden for the ceremony. A large white tent had been erected over a wooden platform and chairs had been arranged in this makeshift chapel. Marc stood at the back, doing his best not to intrude as he photographed the exchange of vows and rings. He caught the moment when Gabe and Alexis first looked at each other as husband and wife, and the joy in their faces left him blinking and wiping furtively at his eyes.

Inside the inn at the wedding dinner, Marc half hoped he would be seated across from his father once more, but Alan and Margie were at the far end of the table. Instead, Marc traded small talk with one of Alexis's cousins and a friend of Aunt Celeste's. He watched for Lacey among the servers, but she remained sequestered in the kitchen—the only damper so far on the day.

After dinner there was dancing. The chairs had been removed from the tent in the garden and the family members who were filling in for the ailing band had set up their instruments nearby. Hundreds of white lights draped the tent, sparkling against the growing darkness.

After the bride and groom waltzed to the first song, the others took their turn. Marc stood on the sidelines, feeling out of place among the happy couples. Uncle Frank and Aunt Audrey danced by, and he spotted Shannon in the arms of Josh. Remembering the photographs he'd taken of them playing Monopoly, he couldn't help but smile.

He spotted his father dancing with Margie. They were smiling at each other. His father looked happy and relaxed, the kind of man Marc might like to know better. As they headed his way, he straightened his suit coat and took a deep breath, then maneuvered among the dancers until he reached them. "May I cut in?" he asked.

Alan looked surprised, but stepped back and

allowed Marc to take his place as Margie's partner. She smiled up at him. "Now this is a pleasure," she said.

"The pleasure's all mine." He quickly discovered Margie was a better dancer than he was, but she covered his missteps nicely. "Where did you learn to dance so well?" he asked.

"Your father and I take lessons," she said. "He didn't want to go at first, but now we both enjoy them."

He filed this away as another tidbit about his father that he hadn't known.

"You look just like the pictures I've seen of Alan when he was younger," she said.

"I do?" He couldn't remember seeing a photograph of his father as a young man. After their divorce, his mother had either hidden or destroyed any photos in her possession

"Oh, yes. You're both so handsome." Margie's expression grew more serious. "He's very proud of you, you know. He tries to buy every magazine or paper where your work appears, and he saves them all."

With each step Marc's image of his father was changing, from the callous monster Marc had made him in his youth to someone more vulnerable.

The song ended and Alan returned to reclaim his wife. "You two looked good out there on the dance floor," he said.

Marc thanked Margie for the dance, then turned to his dad. "How long will you be in Paris?" he asked.

"A few more days. We want to visit the Louvre, see the Mona Lisa—all the things you're supposed to do in Paris. How about you?"

"I'm not sure." How long he stayed depended on a lot of things. "I don't have an assignment due for a while, so I thought I'd stick around for a few more days, at least." He studied the toes of his shoes, suddenly nervous, then raised his head and looked his father in the eye. "I'd like us to get together for dinner while we're both here."

"I'd like that. That would be great." Alan smiled, an expression so full of relief and joy that Marc wanted to look away but he didn't. He kept his gaze fixed on this stranger who was yet so much a part of who he was.

"We have a lot to talk about," Marc said.

Alan nodded. "We do. We'll talk all you want."

Another song started and they were separated again, but Marc knew they'd never be as distant after this as they had been before.

He left the dance floor and wandered back into the inn, where other guests had retreated, as well, to chat in the relative quiet, or to rest tired feet. Taylor sat on a settee, feet up, shoes discarded on the floor, a trio of Marc's younger cousins paying court.

Smiling, he moved past them, headed without even thinking about it for the kitchen.

He found Lacey in the pantry, putting away the silver trays that had been used to serve the wedding dinner. She stood on tiptoe, her back to him, trying to fit a heavy tray into a slot high overhead. "Let me get that for you," he said, stepping forward and taking the tray from her.

She turned to him, her arms going around him as naturally as if they'd known each other all their lives instead of only a few days. When the tray was in place, he kissed her. She still smelled like almonds and vanilla and cinnamon. Or maybe it was only that he was standing next to the spice rack. He smiled at the thought.

"What's so funny?" she asked when they ended the kiss at last.

"Was I laughing?"

"No, but you're smiling. You don't smile often."

He nodded. It was true that he had spent many years being serious. He had not seen a great deal in his life to smile about. But that was changing. "I'm smiling because I'm happy."

Her own smile earned her another kiss. After some time, she wriggled away. "Giselle will come looking for me."

"What's the worst thing she'll do if she finds you kissing in the pantry? She won't fire you, will she?"

Lacey laughed and shook her head. "No. She wouldn't do that." She lowered her voice and leaned closer to him. "When I came in this morning to fetch the spices for the chicken, I caught her and Monsieur Gautier kissing in this very spot."

He looked around them, at the shelves full of cans, bottles, bags and boxes. "I never thought of pantries as romantic before, but I guess they can be."

She took his hand and tugged him out of the little room, into the bigger kitchen. "It was a beautiful wedding, wasn't it?" she asked.

"I can't say I've been to very many weddings, but Gabe and Alexis looked happy and I suppose that's what counts."

"I slipped out into the garden for a few moments during the ceremony," Lacey said. "Alexis was so gorgeous in her gown—and Gabe looked so in love."

He nodded and took her hands in his once more. "Do you believe love can be contagious?"

She laughed again and tried to pull her hands away, but he held them fast. Her expression sobered. "What do you mean?" she asked.

He released her hands and leaned back against the worktable. "I mean, I came to Paris dreading being caught up in the sentiment of a wedding. I hated the idea of romance and thought I'd be bored out of my mind hanging out with a bunch of relatives I hardly knew. I thought photographing a wedding was beneath me. But in these past few days I've found out I was wrong about all of that."

"You were?" She crossed her arms under her

breasts and tilted her head to one side, studying him, her lips parted in a half smile.

He nodded. "I found out I have a great family, one that welcomes and accepts me even when I've been rude and arrogant. Now I think photographing a wedding is a privilege, not a chore. I've spent all week observing Gabe and Alexis and all the other people around me who are in love. And now I think I was wrong about romance, too."

He held out his arms and she came to him, and rested her head on his chest. "Then I do think love can be contagious," she said. "Because I think I've been in love with you since the first night you walked into the kitchen, demanding to be fed."

"I love you, Lacey," he said, kissing the top of her head. "And I'm glad you didn't send me away empty that night. I didn't know it then, but my heart was emptier than my stomach had ever been."

"I'm glad I was able to fill both your stomach and your heart." She kissed him again, then looked up at him, her expression serious. "What are we going to do now?"

"What do you mean?" The kissing had been fine with him, though later he might persuade her to slip back up to his room.

"I still have another six months of study at the Cordon Bleu. And your job takes you all over the world."

"I have a few weeks. I can stay in Paris and we

can see where our feelings lead. Besides, I do know my way to the Paris airport. There's no reason I can't come back here between assignments. And I assume you get vacation here and there."

"You've had a lot of adventure in your life," she said. "Are you sure coming back to the same city over and over will be enough to you?"

"I don't care about the city," he said, cradling her head in his hand. "As long as I come back to the same woman over and over again. Besides, this is new territory for me. Maybe the greatest adventure I've taken yet."

"I guess love is an adventure," she said. One she hoped would last a lifetime for them.

After all, they were in Paris in the springtime— when anything is possible.

Romantic
SUSPENSE

**Sparked by Danger,
Fueled by Passion.**

Mission: Impassioned

A brand-new miniseries begins with

My Spy

By *USA TODAY* bestselling author

Marie Ferrarella

She had to trust him with her life....
It was the most daring mission of Joshua Lazlo's
career: rescuing the prime minister of England's
daughter from a gang of cold-blooded kidnappers.
But nothing prepared the shadowy secret agent
for a fiery woman whose touch ignited something
far more dangerous.

My Spy

#1472

Available July 2007 wherever you buy books!

REQUEST YOUR FREE BOOKS!
2 FREE NOVELS PLUS 2
FREE GIFTS!

HARLEQUIN ROMANCE®

From the Heart, For the Heart

YES! Please send me 2 FREE Harlequin Romance® novels and my 2 FREE gifts. After receiving them, if I don't wish to receive any more books, I can return the shipping statement marked "cancel." If I don't cancel, I will receive 4 brand-new novels every month and be billed just $3.57 per book in the U.S., or $4.05 per book in Canada, plus 25¢ shipping and handling per book and applicable taxes, if any*. That's a savings of over 15% off the cover price! I understand that accepting the 2 free books and gifts places me under no obligation to buy anything. I can always return a shipment and cancel at any time. Even if I never buy another book from Harlequin, the two free books and gifts are mine to keep forever.

114 HDN EEV7   314 HDN EEWK

Name	(PLEASE PRINT)	
Address		Apt.
City	State/Prov.	Zip/Postal Code

Signature (if under 18, a parent or guardian must sign)

Mail to the **Harlequin Reader Service®**:
IN U.S.A.: P.O. Box 1867, Buffalo, NY 14240-1867
IN CANADA: P.O. Box 609, Fort Erie, Ontario L2A 5X3

Not valid to current Harlequin Romance subscribers.

Want to try two free books from another line?
Call 1-800-873-8635 or visit www.morefreebooks.com.

* Terms and prices subject to change without notice. NY residents add applicable sales tax. Canadian residents will be charged applicable provincial taxes and GST. This offer is limited to one order per household. All orders subject to approval. Credit or debit balances in a customer's account(s) may be offset by any other outstanding balance owed by or to the customer. Please allow 4 to 6 weeks for delivery.

Your Privacy: Harlequin is committed to protecting your privacy. Our Privacy Policy is available online at www.eHarlequin.com or upon request from the Reader Service. From time to time we make our lists of customers available to reputable firms who may have a product or service of interest to you. If you would prefer we not share your name and address, please check here. ☐

HR07